Animal Rescue

Tessa looked round at the hole in the bank, the fresh earth – and the sharp metal spade. She shuddered. "Have they been hunting badgers here, then?"

Ned followed her gaze. "It looks as though they've just been digging them out."

"But why?"

Ned shrugged. "Dunno," he admitted. "Somebody must want to get rid." He was silent, apparently thinking. Tessa waited for him to go on, but he just sniffed dismally and turned his head away from her. Suddenly she realized he was crying . . .

Animal Rescue

Bette Paul

Scholastic Children's Books,
Scholastic Publications Ltd,
7–9 Pratt Street, London NW1 0AE, UK

Scholastic Inc.,
555 Broadway, New York, NY 10012-3999, USA

Scholastic Canada Ltd,
123 Newkirk Road, Richmond Hill,
Ontario, Canada L4C 3G5

Ashton Scholastic Pty Ltd,
P O Box 579, Gosford, New South Wales,
Australia

Ashton Scholastic Ltd,
Private Bag 92801, Penrose, Auckland,
New Zealand

First published by Scholastic Children's Books 1994

Copyright © Bette Paul 1994

ISBN 0 590 55815 3

Typeset by TW Typesetting, Midsomer Norton, Avon
Printed by Cox & Wyman Ltd, Reading, Berks.

10 9 8 7 6 5 4 3 2

Chapter 1

"*It's raining, it's pouring
And rotten and boring.*"

Tessa Gostard sang angrily as she skirted the puddles, though it wasn't actually raining and she wasn't really singing. Granny Lila would have said she was shouting and told her to shut up; but Granny Lila also said a little sing-song made you feel better than a little cry. Huh! Tessa stopped the singing/shouting and stood silent for a moment, to see if Granny Lila's treatment had worked. It hadn't.

Tessa sniffed hard, wiped her eyes with the

back of her hand and gazed gloomily along the empty lane to the deserted village green. It was so quiet she could even hear herself breathing; and it was so lonely it made her want to weep. So much for Granny Lila's sing-song cure.

She'd promised Granny Lila, when they parted two days ago, that she'd try hard to settle into her new home in the country with Dad.

"Your father's making a fresh start," Gran had told her. "You're a lucky girl, Tessa, you'll have a new home, a new car and some nice new friends."

But not a new mum, Tessa thought now. And the home is an ugly red house, the car is an old green Forestry van and where are all those new friends? I haven't seen anybody except Dad since the removal men left two days ago. She scowled and stamped her welly into the mud.

"It's lonely!" Splosh.

"It's boring!" Splosh.

"And it's far too quiet!" she yelled down the

lane and stamped her feet in the puddle once more: splosh, splosh, splosh!

Well, that was fun – almost. Tessa allowed herself a small grin and prepared to splash all the way to the Post Office, where she was going to buy eggs for tea.

"Eggs – from a Post Office?" she'd asked Dad. "You don't buy eggs at a Post Office."

"You do when you want to make eggs-on-post," he'd answered. But Tessa had refused to smile. She just took the money off him, pulled on her wellies and slammed out of the back door. She stomped down the path without looking back, thinking how different it would have been if only her dad had still worked at the parks department in London, and if only her mum hadn't gone back to Canada, and if only she didn't have to choose between them.

Tessa was feeling tearful now, rather than angry, so she walked on in gloomy silence. Which was why she suddenly heard a small, weird sound like a clockwork toy.

"Quaaaak, quaaa, quaa . . ."

Tessa looked down the lane and saw something little and low, crouching on the roadside, shuffling towards her.

"Quaaaak!" it said again, and even Tessa recognized the call.

But she could hardly recognize the creature. It was covered in mud, splattered with blood and trailing one wing. When it arrived at her feet it collapsed and settled on her muddy welly.

"Quaa . . ." It was too weak even to finish its cry.

Ugh! Tessa pulled a face and stared down at the bedraggled little creature. She'd often seen ducks like this one, on the lake in the park where her dad used to work. But she'd never been close to one – never wanted to. She shuddered, closed her eyes and prepared to step over the soggy mess. But the bird made another attempt to quack, though it came out as the slightest chirrup, and Tessa opened her eyes and looked again, more closely.

She could see that it was breathing very fast and its trailing wing twitched now and then, as if trying to fly. Even as she watched, the duck raised its little head and cheeped weakly, and Tessa saw spots of blood oozing from a wound on its neck. Its bright little eye blinked up at her, then suddenly shut tight.

"Oh, lordy me," Tessa said aloud. "What on earth shall I do with you?" And the tears in her eyes were not only for herself now.

She thought about running back to the cottage to fetch Dad. But she couldn't leave the animal out in the middle of the lane. Only that very morning she'd seen a posh white Range Rover tearing past Delves Cottage. It would only take one fast car to finish the duck off completely. She shuddered at the thought: she'd have to move the creature somehow, whether she liked it or not.

Tessa bent over the duck. It didn't stir. Perhaps it's too ill to be afraid, she thought. But even if I dare to pick it up, how can I carry it?

She looked around for a discarded plastic bag, perhaps, or even a newspaper. But the country lane was not like her city street; there was no litter. Tessa looked up for inspiration and noticed that the rain had stopped, leaving the air quite still and warm.

So she took off her denim jacket and gently dropped it over the duck. When she rolled the jacket over and picked it up she could feel the bird inside it, shivering. She held it close to her chest; its heart was beating very fast and fluttery. Tessa peered down anxiously; what if she'd done it more harm by picking it up? But it snuggled into the warmth of Tessa's body, chirruping gently, as if it was comfortable.

For the first time since she'd left the city, Tessa forgot to feel sorry for herself. She held the duck close and walked carefully, avoiding the puddles now, towards the village. She could have taken it back to Dad, but he was no expert: trees were his job. It was a vet she needed – and where better to find a vet than in the country, she thought, hurrying now to the village green.

Well, there was a pub, a butcher's shop and a Post Office, apart from the cottages and houses scattered around the green. No vets. What should she do with the duck?

The lady at the Post Office helped. "From Delves Cottage, aren't you?" she said, even though Tessa hadn't told her. "Just take the poor thing over to Nora's Place – round the back of the pub there."

Nora's Place? Tessa was puzzled. It sounded more like a café than a vet's. She carried her burden carefully along the village street and round the back of the pub. The duck stirred a little now and then against her chest and when Tessa felt it move, a great surge went through her. Part of her wanting the duck to be all right, another part worrying in case it leapt out of her arms and killed itself.

"Oh, come on, Nora's, whatever you are, wherever you are. Help!"

She stood looking for Nora's, but all she could see was a collection of sheds and a rough, steep field with a couple of donkeys in it. She leaned on the gate clutching her blood-stained parcel and wondered what to do next.

A load of hay walked from one of the sheds towards her. She watched in amazement as it staggered down the hill. But then she saw two legs sticking out below and suddenly the whole load shot into the open doorway of one of the huts. A boy with a pitchfork turned to face her. He was a big boy, tall as herself, but much heavier, with a large head and a blank expression. He looked at her without speaking.

"Hey, you! Know anything about a place called Nora's Place?" she asked, rather loudly.

And he nodded, several times, up, down, up, down.

Just my luck, thought Tessa, in despair. I've found the village idiot, first time out.

"I've got a wounded duck," she said, speaking

loudly and slowly so that the boy could understand.

Nod, nod. "Mallard?" he asked, as if it
mattered.

This boy was obviously quite mad, thought
Tessa. She remembered the notices round the
park lake back home, with pictures of the birds
that lived there. She'd gazed at them dozens of
times while she waited for Dad to finish work.
Only in a half-hearted, bored sort of way: bird
watching was not good for street cred.

"Mallard," she repeated. Well, it sounded
familiar. "Could be."

The boy began to look interested. Nod, nod.
Then, "Male?" he asked.

Really, it was as if they were doing a quiz,
Tessa thought impatiently.

"The point is," she said, slowly, as if address-
ing a child, "that it's hurt and I'm trying to find
this Nora's Place. Now, do you know where it
is?"

The boy didn't reply. He just came down,

opened the gate for her and set off across the field. He seemed to expect Tessa to follow. Normally, Tessa Gostard would not be seen dead following a mere boy, but she had to do something about the poor duck. She hitched up her burden, sniffed scornfully and plodded up the wet field after the village idiot.

He led the way to a bulky old camper van, parked at the top of the hill. There wasn't another building in sight; even the village had disappeared behind the steep slope of the field. Tessa stood for a moment and looked all round. What was this idiot boy playing at? She should have known better than to trust him.

But the "idiot boy" reached up, slid open the door of the camper van and clambered inside. Tessa waited but he didn't offer to help her. Breathing hard, she heaved herself and her duck after him.

For a moment she stood quite still and looked all round in amazement. The camping van was obviously not used for camping: it looked more like a mobile shop than a home. It was lined with small shelves stacked with bottles, jars and packets. Along one side ran a work-top, with a sink and a couple of gas burners let into it. At the end of the bench sat a woman with her back to them.

"Shut that door, Ned. How many more times?" she said, in a slightly northern voice.

The boy reached behind Tessa and slid the door across. "It's a mallard," he told the woman. "Male." He seemed to think this was something special.

"Where?" The woman turned now and looked at Tessa through big round glasses, then down at her burden. "Right," she smiled. "Let's have a look at him."

The boy gave Tessa a gentle shove and she unrolled her jacket and spilled the duck out on to the work-top. She was surprised to see him stand up and look around with quick bright eyes.

"Come along, my lovely," the woman said

gently. She snapped on a strong little lamp above the bench and scooped up the duck.

"Careful, he's injured," said Tessa, surprised to find herself wincing with the duck's pain.

"Shhhhhh," whispered the boy. "Nora's the expert."

Tessa flushed with annoyance, partly at the boy for bossing her about and partly at herself for bossing this woman, who obviously *was* an expert. She now had the duck splayed out under the lamp and was feeling round his body with strong, rather dirty fingers.

So she is Nora, thought Tessa. And this van must be her Place. An odd sort of place for a vet. Odd sort of vet, come to think of it. Tessa had a vision of a fresh-faced young man in tweeds and a waxed jacket and green wellies. A small, bespectacled woman in an ancient cardigan and trainers was not Tessa's idea of a vet.

Nora was muttering to herself all the time she examined the injured creature. "There, there, my lovely . . . let's have a look at you . . . still, now . . . all right . . ." As if he knew she was going to help, the duck relaxed and stayed quite still in her grasp. "Bit of rest, bit of cleaning," said Nora. "Pass that washing-up liquid, Ned."

Tessa watched fascinated as the clean green feathers emerged from the mud and blood, as if Nora was re-creating the bird. And suddenly it was the only thing in the world she wanted. It was, after all, the first and only friend she'd found, out in the country.

"Thanks," she said as Nora appeared to finish washing the bird. "I'll take him home now."

The boy shook his head. "No," he said, in the slow, broad tones of the Derbyshire Dales. "You can't do that."

"It's all right," she said, sharply. This Ned had quite a knack of annoying her. "My dad'll pay the bill."

Nora was smoothing the bird's wing-feathers with cotton wool. "He'll have to stay here until he's quite better," she explained. Then, as Tessa scowled with disappointment, "Would you like to hold him?"

And she scooped up the glistening duck and put him into Tessa's arms. As she cradled him against her and stroked his back, he lifted his head and chirruped softly, as if he knew her. Tessa blinked back tears.

Ned shuffled across with a straw-lined box. "There you are!" he said, as if that settled any argument, and Tessa reluctantly tucked the bird in.

"I'll put him in with his mate," said Ned.

"You don't know that she's his mate," said Nora.

"Must be. Wouldn't have two brought in on one day."

He speaks to Nora just the same way he spoke to me, thought Tessa. Bossy-boots, not village idiot.

"Where did you find him?" Nora asked Tessa.

"Wandering up the lane to Delves Cottage."

Ned was nodding vigorously now, up and

down, up and down. "Looking for his mate," he said.

Tessa peered into the box. The duck had tucked his head right round on to his glossy back now and gone to sleep.

"He's right enough now," said Nora. She turned to Tessa. "But what about you? Your jacket's in a mess. Give it here – I'll sponge it clean."

Tessa suddenly remembered why she'd come down to the village in the first place. "I must do the shopping and get back home," she said. "Dad'll be worried."

"Here," Nora passed her a car phone. "I think we can regard this as a business call, don't you?" she smiled. "You talk to your dad while I clean your jacket and Ned'll make us all a cup of coffee."

Tessa enjoyed surprising Dad by her call.

"I'm glad you're making friends," he said, before she put the phone down. "See you soon – don't forget the eggs!"

"See you soon!" Tessa grinned, happily. "And don't forget the eggcups!"

It was friendly, sitting in the van with mugs of coffee and nutty cookies while the mallard slept. Tessa chatted to Nora and told her all about the problems of settling into Delves Cottage.

". . . and Dad's so busy sorting out all his precious books that we haven't even found the eggcups yet."

Nora laughed. "I'll send some fresh eggs back with you; he'll have to find the eggcups then!"

Ned didn't say much, but when Tessa's coat was dry he took her down to one of the huts, where they collected the eggs and put the sleeping mallard in a run with the little brown duck which he believed was his mate.

Then Ned took her on a tour of the huts and the field, where she met several rabbits, some hens, a flock of geese, a couple of goats and the donkeys.

"Are they all yours?" Tessa asked, edging nervously away from a nuzzling donkey.

Ned nodded, this time with a quiet smile.

"But who takes care of them all?"

"Me. Well, Mum looks after the poorly ones." He nodded in the direction of the van.

"You mean Nora, she's your mum?"

He nodded in just the same way as he had when they'd first met, up, down, up, down.

"Is she a vet?" Nod, nod. Pause.

"Just emergencies, like," he explained. "Can't afford a practice of our own."

Tessa noted the "our"; she didn't know whether to be amused or impressed. She looked all round at the battered little huts in the scrubby field. "So this is Nora's Place?" she said, vaguely disappointed.

For the first time since they'd met, Ned looked straight at her, challenging any criticism. Nod, nod, nod, very firmly.

"Well . . . I'd better be getting home," said Tessa, awkwardly.

Home! As she said it, Tessa suddenly remembered Granny Lila's words: "A new home, new friends . . ."

They walked along Delves Lane together, the egg-basket between them. They didn't talk. Tessa had lots of questions she wanted to ask, but she already knew that Ned didn't do much talking. So she contented herself with stepping out, measuring her strides to match his.

I'm going to my new home, thought Tessa, with six new eggs and one new friend.

And she hoped Dad had found the eggcups.

Chapter 2

Dad was delighted with the eggs; he even found the eggcups, and he was obviously relieved that Tessa had found a friend. Tessa wasn't at all sure about the friend – for a start, Ned didn't exactly sparkle: he was very quiet, rather serious, and then, well, he was a boy. Tessa wondered what the girls back home would say if they knew that the only friend she had was a boy. Tessa's gang had very firm views about boys, none of them good.

But she never saw anyone else. And as she would have to go down to Nora's Place every

morning to see her mallard and as Ned seemed
to assume she'd want to help him with the
other animals, they were rather thrown together. So perhaps that was all right, then;
anyway, she could always tell the girls she now
had a job!

A few days later, Tessa ran down Delves Lane
to Nora's Place feeling so amazingly happy that
she was singing one of Granny Lila's silly songs:

Up in the morning underneath the ground,
Looking for the clutterbucks that never can be
found
As long as I remember
I never shall forget
To bring me umberdumber
When it turns out wet.

Tessa warbled away, slightly off-key, and
suddenly felt so joyful that she did a welly-boot
dance right down the middle of the lane.

"Get out of my way!"

She jumped as a loud motor horn sounded
just behind her. She turned and saw a man

leaning out of a shiny white Range Rover. "Keep on th' grass verge, you stupid girl!" he shouted. He had a big red face and pale, bulgy eyes, Tessa noticed as she jumped back.

"I'm not stupid," she shouted up at him. "You were going too fast!" It was true, but she knew Dad wouldn't approve of cheek.

Neither did the driver of the Range Rover; he scowled down at her and pulled off so fast that the tyres threw up gravel which stung as it hit her legs.

Where did he come from? Tessa wondered. Delves Lane was a dead end, leading only to their cottage and a bridle-path through the woods. Tessa watched the Range Rover disappear round the green. Well, she'd watch out for that man again; she didn't like him, whoever he was. Ned would know, she realized; she'd ask him.

But it was some time before she got the chance. Ned was in the shed sorting out the animal feeds when she arrived.

"Hi!" she greeted him. "Can I go and see the mallards?"

Ned just grunted as he lifted a heavy bucket to the door.

Tessa hesitated; she didn't even know whether Ned's grunt meant "hello" or "push off!" Before she could make up her mind, he spoke again.

"For the ducks." He held out a bag of bird-food and very nearly smiled at her. "Then the rabbits." He indicated a sack of pellets.

Back home, Tessa would have told him what to do with his pellets. But here, things were different; Ned was harmless enough and she'd nothing else to do. She took the bag and plodded over to the ducks.

The male mallard was very handsome now with his glossy green head held high and his shiny feathers looking as if they'd been polished. His mate followed him all round the field, brown and downy. They kept calling as if looking for something.

"What do they want?" Tessa asked Ned as he passed on his way to the goats.

"To be off," he said, briefly.

Tessa stood clutching the bag of food close to her just as she'd once clutched the mallard. A wave of desolation swept over her, like it had the day Mum left for Canada; the day Dad lost his job; the day they left the city and she lost all her friends. Now she was even going to lose her mallard!

"Will they go far?" she asked, in a small, choked voice.

Ned stopped, put down the bucket, and looked at her hard. "Debdale Water," he said. "Won't take us long in the van."

Us? Had Ned invited her to go to Debdale? Tessa wished he'd make things clear; he always seemed to talk in shorthand.

"Donkey time," he said, tugging at the bucket. Tessa moved alongside and they took half the handle each, staggering up the field to the donkey shed.

Tessa was not very keen on mucking out the donkey shed. She was not very keen on feeding the donkeys either. With their sharp little hooves and their big brown teeth, they seemed to threaten her.

"You can have a ride when we're done," said Ned, as if offering her a treat.

Tessa shuddered. "No thanks," she said firmly. "I'll go and do the rabbits now."

She took a bag of pellets from the shed and ran across to the edge of the meadow to the rabbit runs. Rabbits were safer than donkeys.

"I'd rather ride my bike than get up on one of those donkeys," she told the biggest rabbit.

"Who you talking to?"

The voice made her jump and she scattered pellets everywhere. She looked all around but there was only Ned across by the donkey shed and he was saying nothing. She was just about to collect the spilled pellets when the voice made her jump again.

"You allus talk to rabbits?" it said. This time

25

Tessa followed the sound upwards and saw the fat round face of a boy hanging on top of the fence like a low moon. He had pale cheeks and light, bulging eyes that reminded Tessa of someone but she couldn't think who it was. She stared at the face and the face stared back.

"You Noddy's cousin or summat?" He spoke in a thick, nasal voice, as if he was full of cold.

Tessa had no idea who Noddy was – he certainly wasn't her cousin: she had no cousins, but that was none of this boy's business. She turned her back to the fence and bent to pick up the pellets and throw them into the rabbit runs. She was very irritated by the boy; he made her feel stupid, just like that man in the Range Rover that morning. And Tessa Gostard, smart and streetwise, was not going to let this little bumpkin make her feel like that.

"Ignore it and it'll go away," her Gran always told her when she had an irritating itch. That's what she'd do: ignore him and he'd go away.

Deliberately, she tossed her head, sniffed loudly, and bent over the rabbits.

"You on your holidays, like?" The boy ignored her ignoring him.

"You always so nosey, like?" Tessa replied, stung into speaking to this irritating gnat of a boy.

"You're from Delves Cottage, aren't you? Me dad said somebody'd moved in up there. Some incomers, he said, from London. Me dad allus knows what's going on. Me dad owns that field, you know," he said, as if she should be impressed.

The boy's face was very red now; Tessa guessed he was stretching up to see over and, as he hitched up to get a firmer grip, she caught a glimpse of a red bow tie peeping over the edge of the fence. It seemed an odd thing to be wearing, in the country. Still, they'd hardly be into top fashion out here, would they?

Tossing her head and sniffing once more, she picked up her bucket, glared up at him and moved off, feeling his bulgy eyes watching her all the way.

"Who's the boy?" she asked Ned.

"Mmmm?" He looked up vaguely. "Where?"

Tessa looked back to the fence but the other boy had gone. "Fat face, with a cold," she said. "Leaning over the fence nattering about somebody called . . ."

"Noddy," Ned said very quietly, nodding to himself.

Too late, Tessa realized who Noddy was. To her annoyance she blushed but Ned didn't seem to mind. He just bent down to pick up one of the donkey's hooves and scraped round it with his knife.

"Skilbeck," he said.

Tessa peered at the hoof. "Is that a disease?" she asked.

Ned grinned and started on another hoof. "Jason Skilbeck's a pain but he's not a disease." He frowned and nodded seriously over the hoof. "He's the boy you saw across there."

Tessa was all agog to hear how Jason Skilbeck was a pain; she and her friends had long conversations about the painful boys they knew. But Ned didn't say any more. They worked on together in silence, Ned mucking out, Tessa filling up the stables and hutches with fresh straw.

By the time Nora came back from her rounds, all the animals were clean and fed but their keepers were both cold and hungry.

"Come into the van and get warm," said Nora. "Put the kettle on, Ned; I've brought some fresh baps from the Post Office."

It was only when she was halfway through her hot chocolate and buttered bap that Tessa remembered the man up the lane. When she told Ned and Nora about him they both looked gloomy.

"Gary Skilbeck," said Nora.

"Two in one morning," said Ned. And he told his mum about Tessa's meeting with Jason.

"Father and son," Nora sighed. "Ah well, you can't move in this village without coming across the Skilbecks."

"Or crossing them," said Ned. And Tessa had the feeling that he'd already crossed one Skilbeck or other.

But before she could ask any questions, Nora stood up. "Well, what about these mallards then?" And it was Tessa's turn to feel gloomy.

But they had such fun catching the mallards that even Tessa was laughing by the time they climbed back into the van. They tucked the birds into a basket and fastened themselves into the front seat with Nora.

They were all very quiet on the journey to Debdale. Nora concentrated on driving up the steep, twisty lanes; Ned, as usual, said nothing; and Tessa sat sunk in gloom, thinking about losing the mallards, losing all her friends, all the fun of city life, her mum, even Granny Lila, now settled into her very tiny old-people's flat, with no room for her. Suddenly she remembered how she'd promised Granny Lila that she'd look after Dad and here she was, out with her friends, and he was left all on his own. Tessa was so deep in her worries that she didn't even notice when the van pulled up.

"Here we are!" Nora pulled off the road down to a stony patch, like a beach, at the edge of the water. You all right, Tessa? Did the twisty ride make you feel sick?"

Tessa shook her head. "I was just thinking I ought to get back for dinner," she said. "Dad's expecting me."

Nora smiled and handed her the car phone. "Ring him," she said. "We'll get moving and let the birds out."

So Tessa sat in the van listening to the phone ringing at Delves Cottage. Obviously Dad wasn't at home. Off somewhere, managing quite well without her. Dad could manage quite well without anyone. Not like her – she needed lots of people, lots of noise and fun. Tessa sighed and watched the pale sunshine playing across Debdale Water. The trees along the shore were just slightly fringed with green, and beyond them the hills rose brown and dark. It was very beautiful, even Tessa had to admit, and so quiet that she suddenly jumped as the mallards waddled down the beach, squawking loudly.

"Are they all right?" Tessa asked, when she joined Nora and Ned outside.

Ned nodded. Noddy, thought Tessa – that's why they call him that. He uses nods instead of words.

Nora smiled. "Once they take to the water, we'll know they're settled," she said, perching on the top step of the camper. "They won't take long now," she said.

The little brown female was already in the water, swimming frantically round in circles and making little chirruping noises as if purring. Her mate sat on the bank and watched her but he didn't offer to join her yet.

Nora peeled an orange and shared it amongst

the three of them. They sat on the camper steps, nibbling quietly, and watching the mallards.

As if he'd learnt from his mate, the male mallard stood up now and stretched his neck forward, shifting his wings experimentally.

"Oh, look!" exclaimed Tessa.

"Sshhhhh!" Ned spoke sharply. Tessa flushed and turned her attention to the duck. Only just in time. Almost running down the bank, he set off, wings outstretched, then flew up into the air above the lake. It was so quiet here that Tessa could even hear the beat of his wings as he pulled upwards. Free! thought Tessa, remembering her mum, flying off to her new job in Canada.

"But what about his mate?" Tessa whispered this time.

"Watch!" Ned ordered, nodding and humming happily to himself.

The male mallard swooped round and down on to the water, as if skiing, and softly paddled

up to his mate. Then they both disappeared into the reeds.

"Gone," said Tessa sadly.

"Only house-hunting," smiled Nora. "They'll start nesting now and later she'll lay her eggs. We'll be back to see how they're getting on. This is our favourite picnic spot, isn't it, Ned?"

Nod, nod. "There'll be chicks later in the season," said Ned.

Nora smiled and patted Tessa's shoulder. "Come on, chick, it's time you were back in your nest."

Tessa laughed at Nora's joke; she was no longer sad to see the mallards go. They were settling down to live in a lovely spot – a bit like Dad and herself, she thought. And she felt so happy to have seen the birds settled that she actually enjoyed the drive home. She watched the road weaving up from the lake, through the woods and out over the hills to Delver. After a night of rain, the countryside looked freshly washed, sparkling now and then in the fitful sunshine. The distant hills were dappled as the wind scattered clouds. It was so beautiful that even Tessa didn't want to chat.

Ned, of course, said nothing, until they pulled in at Delves Cottage. Then he let out a groan. "Oh, no!"

Tessa followed his gaze up the path where her dad was washing his boots. Jason Skilbeck was standing watching him.

"Now then, Ned, don't be unkind," said Nora.

Tessa was too worried about having been away too long to bother about Jason Skilbeck. "Sorry I'm so late, Dad," she called as she hurried up the path. "I did ring but you weren't here."

Dad looked up from his boots. "It's all right, Tess," he said. "A friend of yours told me you'd gone off with Ned and his mum so I knew you were safe."

Tessa stopped halfway up the garden path. A friend? Jason fat-face Skilbeck? She hesitated and turned back to look at Ned. He scowled down at her and said something to his mother. Nora waved and the van pulled away.

"You should have brought Ned and his mum in for tea," said Dad. "I got some fresh-baked baps up at the Post Office today."

Tessa watched the van disappearing down the lane and remembered Nora's words: "You can't move in this village without coming across a Skilbeck." And Ned had made one of his quiet jokes. What was it?

"Tessa!" Dad was shouting now. "Stop day-dreaming and ask your friend indoors."

Tessa looked blank.

"Jason," explained Dad. "He did tell me where you were, you know. The least we can do is offer him some tea."

But Jason was looking at his large, complicated watch. "I gotter go now," he said. "She never lets me stay to tea. Not with . . . er . . . strangers."

Tessa glared at him. She knew what he'd

nearly said, although she wasn't sure what it meant: "incomer" he'd called her that morning, and it was an insult, she felt sure.

But Dad just nodded calmly. "Quite right too," he said to Jason. "I'll ring your mother next time – bring your boots and we'll go up the woods."

To Tessa's relief, Jason looked doubtful, though whether about Mr Gostard talking to his mother or walking in the woods, she couldn't tell. She contented herself with glowering silently.

"See yer, then," he said hastily. And he ran off up the path.

"Come on then, Tess, what are we going to have for dinner – or is it teatime now?" said Dad.

Tessa sighed. At home she'd have rushed round to the chippy, or the pizza place, or the Chinese take-away. Or better still, Granny Lila would be round with a pie. But here in Delver, they had to cook every meal themselves.

"Beans on toast?" she said.

Dad groaned. "I don't know what it is about beans," he said. "I loved them Monday, liked them Tuesday, didn't mind them Wednesday but today I've suddenly gone off them."

Tessa grinned. "OK then, we'll have a change."

"Great! And what does the chef recommend today?"

"Beans on a bap," said Tessa. "A local speciality."

Chapter 3

To Tessa's relief, it wasn't Jason Skilbeck who came up to the woods with Dad; it was Ned. On the last day of the holidays, Dad took them both to see his "office" out there.

For once, Tessa was quite happy to leave the animals to Nora; it was much more fun to be striding along the bridle-path on a bright spring morning listening to the wind sighing in the branches and sniffing the damp, dank scent of the leaf mould. She skipped on the bouncy grass track and ran ahead to find Dad's cabin.

When she found it she was less than thrilled.

"It's not like the log cabin in that book we read," she said, staring at the long green hut.

Dad laughed a deep, rumbling laugh, and his teeth shone from the shadows of his dark beard. "You mean *The Little House in the Big Woods*. No thank you; I did all that in my young days back in Canada," he said. "This is a real PortaKabin with all mod cons."

Once inside, Tessa could see what he meant. The PortaKabin was both an office and a lab: it had a big desk, filing cabinets and a big black swivel chair at one end; but the other end was like a science lab, with a work-top bench, a sink and glass cupboards full of apparatus. "Is this where you'll be working?" she asked her father.

"Not often," he answered. "I'll be out learning about the woodlands at first. It's all very different from my work in the city parks, you know. Starting Monday, I have a lot to learn."

Tessa was quiet; she suddenly realized that on Monday she had to go to her new school. She'd be stuck in a classroom full of strangers whilst he was out in the forest, miles away. Of course he had often been miles away in the city, but there were buses and tube trains and she could always get in touch if she needed him. But how could she do that in the wilds of Delves Wood?

As if he knew what she was thinking, Ned said, "How do you keep in touch with the office when you're out in the woods?"

Tessa's dad grinned. "I never realized that the countryside was so high tech," he said. "I have my Cellnet phone, and there's an answering machine in here."

"So I can ring you when your tea's ready?" said Tessa.

"You won't have to. I'll be home for tea before you've finished helping Ned with the animals," Dad promised. He shuffled through the papers and letters on his desk. "I'll just look through this lot, then we'll . . ."

He was muttering away to himself as he read and Tessa knew he'd forgotten them. "He'll be ages now," she told Ned. "Come on, you can show me your famous woods." She was being a bit sarcastic; she'd heard Ned telling Dad about the woods so often that she was actually a bit jealous. Ned never talked to her about anything, she thought.

Ignoring the sarcastic tone, Ned led the way and they slipped off unnoticed. The trees in this part of the forest were the oldest and tallest. They had long, grey trunks which arched upwards like the pillars in a cathedral. The wind sighed and moved through the graceful branches.

"Like the sea," Tessa was whispering, though she didn't know why.

"That's because they're *beech* trees," said Ned.

Tessa laughed so much that she tripped over a tree-root. "Ow!" she squealed as she dropped down into a hole on the other side of the tree.

"Shhhh!" warned Ned, who was always sure-footed and silent.

"But I might have broken something," Tessa

said indignantly. She rubbed her shins and moved her legs cautiously.

"Come on, get up," said Ned. He offered her a hand but before she stood up she kicked out again just to check her feet, and clang! there was a noise as her foot hit something metal.

"What's that?" Tessa jumped up quickly.

Ned immediately got down and scrabbled through the loose earth around the hole. He was so busy sifting through it he forgot all about Tessa.

Just like Dad with his flipping papers, she thought. "Oh, come on, Ned," she said. "There won't be any buried treasure here."

Ned didn't answer. Instead he reached down into the hole and pulled out a long spade. He stood up, grinned, and held it out as if it was real treasure.

"Well?" asked Tessa, unimpressed. She'd found better treasure in the fruit machine at the chippy back home.

"Don't you know what it is?" asked Ned.

"'Course I do," said Tessa. "Some dumbo's left a spade in the middle of the woods. I might have cut my leg open. Really, I thought you country folk were . . ."

"Shut up," said Ned. "And come and look down here."

He was down in the hole now, getting filthy, sniffing and peering round the edges. "Yes . . . mm . . . must be . . ." he nodded and muttered.

Tessa watched, reminded of Ratty, scraping away in the snow in the Wild Wood. Well, she wasn't going to be silly little Moley, and Ned wasn't going to discover the entrance to Mr Badger's—

"There!" said Ned, with quiet excitement in his voice.

"What? Where?" asked Tessa, forgetting to keep aloof and jumping into the loose earth around the hole.

"Shhhh, steady on," said Ned. "You'll disturb them even more."

"Who?" asked Tessa, looking round wildly.

"Badgers."

"You mean like *The Wind in the Willows*?" Tessa couldn't believe this. There was Ned/Ratty, scrabbling away in the earth. Here was Tessa/Moley, falling down on to a piece of metal. And now, it seemed, they really were at Mr Badger's door.

"I mean like badgers," said Ned. "This is a sett."

"But badgers wouldn't have a spade," said Tessa.

Ned raised his eyebrows; Tessa felt suddenly stupid.

"Look, badgers dig with their claws – right?" Ned spoke like a teacher starting a lesson.

Tessa nodded. "Right," she agreed. "So what about the spade?"

"Somebody's been digging them out." Ned's face tightened with anger.

"Oh, so people collect them?" asked Tessa, brightly.

Ned stared as if he couldn't believe her.

"No," he said. "But they gas them and poison them, and set their dogs on them . . ."

Tessa was horrified. "What for?" she asked. "Are badgers dangerous?"

"No they are not!" Ned said firmly. "They're peaceful animals who do no harm to anybody."

"So why is everybody after them?"

Ned sighed. "Not everybody," he said. "Just a few nutters who think it's good sport."

Tessa looked round at the hole in the bank, the fresh earth – and the sharp metal spade. She shuddered. "Have they been hunting badgers here, then?"

Ned followed her gaze. "It looks as though they've just been digging them out."

"But why?"

Ned shrugged. "Dunno," he admitted. "Somebody must want to get rid." He was silent, apparently thinking. Tessa waited for him to go on, but he just sniffed dismally and turned his head away from her. Suddenly she realized he was crying!

Back home, Tessa would have been embarrassed by a boy in tears, or even triumphant, if she'd caused them. But Ned was different, though she still didn't understand why he was so upset.

"We'd better get back," she said, softly. She waited at the edge of the bank while Ned collected himself.

"Hey . . . look," she said suddenly – and far too loudly, she realized. "There are tracks in the mud on this side."

Ned heaved a juddering sigh and scrambled out of the hole. Together they examined the tracks, not hearing Dad's call.

"What are you two up to?" he asked, looking down from the bridle-track. "Don't disappear like that. You could get lost in these woods, you know."

"Badgers, Dad," said Tessa. "Somebody's been . . . moving them." She knew Ned wouldn't want to explain, not just yet. Dad looked at the spade, then at the tracks.

"Mmmm – four-wheel drive, Land Rover, I think. New tyres, too . . ."

Tessa remembered that first morning on Delves Lane, the morning of the mallard – and the Range Rover. "You can hardly move in this village without coming across a Skilbeck," Nora had said.

"The Skilbecks have got a Range Rover," said Tessa.

Ned looked at her. "Them and a few hundred others," he said. "Including the Forestry workers." He looked at Mr Gostard and handed him the spade.

"Well, this isn't a Forestry Commission spade," said Tessa's dad. "Look." He pointed to an orange squiggle on the back of the handle. "Our stuff's all stamped with a crown, deep into the wood."

They stood peering at the mark. "Looks like a snake," said Tessa.

"Well, nobody's working in this part of the wood just now but I'll make a point of coming this way next week, to keep an eye on things." Dad flung the spade back into the hole.

"Are you going to leave it there?" asked Ned.

"Well, we don't want whoever left it to know it's been discovered, do we?"

"Well, they might . . ." Ned swallowed hard. "Might come back." That was all he said but Dad knew what he meant.

"I hope they do," he said grimly. "I don't start work up here until Monday, but I'll keep a lookout all weekend."

"Hey – can I use your binoculars?" Tessa said eagerly. "I can keep watch from my bedroom window all night!"

"You won't see anything if you make that din," said Dad. "And anyway, I can't have you staying up all night; Granny Lila would have my guts for garters!"

Tessa giggled at Granny Lila's favourite threat. But Ned looked gloomy. "Tessa's right, though," he said, kicking the earth back over the spade. "If anybody is after the badgers, they'll come at night – that's just the time we need to keep watch."

"I'll take a turn up here tonight," Dad promised. "There's no point hanging about here now, though – the badgers won't come out and I don't think their hunters will be back just yet."

And as they walked back to the van, Ned told them about the badgers of Delves Wood and how they lived there even before humans came to settle in the valley, long before the building of Delver. Tessa had never heard Ned talk so much. Dad listened in silence and squeezed Tessa's hand every time she started to ask a question. It wasn't until they climbed into the van that Ned was silent once more.

"That was really interesting, Ned," said Dad. "Thanks for all the information. I'll do a deal: you teach me all about the woods and I'll see what I can do about keeping an eye on the badgers. Right?"

"Right," Ned agreed. Nod, nod, nodding, a little more happily now.

When they got back to Delves Cottage they had to sit outside and clean the mud off their boots. They were just going indoors when they heard a persistent blast of a hooter echoing up the lane from the green.

Ned shot up. "'Scuse me." He dropped his muddy boots and thrust his feet into battered old trainers. "Library." He nodded over towards the green.

"A library – in Delver?" Tessa exclaimed. "I've never seen it." She padded down to the gate in her socks and peered down the lane, looking for the big public building she'd apparently missed. But there was nothing on the green except for a huge blue van.

"That's it," said Ned, coming up behind her. "Every Wednesday."

"A library in a van?" asked Tessa, more scornfully than she intended.

"Good idea!" Dad frowned down at her. "We'll go and join," he said firmly.

So whilst Ned went off to get his books,

Tessa and Dad climbed up into the library van. Tessa was amazed to discover that in a space no bigger than their removal van was a complete little library, with shelves and shelves of books and even a librarian's desk, just behind the driving seat. Dad stood there to fill in their forms and order some books for next week.

Tessa sniffed in the scent of books and papers and remembered her library back in the city, where the children had a huge room with bean-bags to sit on at storytime, when the librarian read to them; and where there was a reference section which Tessa often used for school pro-jects. She looked along the narrow passageway between the shelves; no chance of sitting on the floor to hear a story, no comfy chairs to sit in to read all by yourself, no tables for homework. Tessa sniffed scornfully.

But she did see something that pleased her. At the far end of the passage, three girls stood, huddled over the children's books. At last! she thought, rushing towards them.

"Hi!" she said. "I'm Tessa Gostard. Right?"

Instead of answering, they merely stared at her for a moment, then the tallest girl made a very strange noise, a sort of explosive snort. Tessa recognized it immediately; she'd made that sound many a time when somebody started giggling in assembly. Tessa looked behind her, but there was only Dad at the front of the bus. For a moment she was puzzled. Then she realized that the girl was giggling at him, and at her, too.

She flushed pink with fury and she scowled at the girls. "What's so funny, then?" she asked, taking a threatening step towards them. Then Ned, puffing hard and carrying a great pile of books, clambered into the van.

Tessa turned and waved to him. "Hi, Ned," she called, rather too loudly. That'd show those stupid girls that she didn't need to be friends with them. She tossed her head and glared at them.

But the girls just nudged each other now and

turned to stare at Ned. He appeared not to have noticed them. He was busy sorting out a heap of books and going through a list with the librarian.

Then Dad, Ned and the librarian chatted about the cuts in book supplies and Tessa was left marooned with the gigglers. The tallest one, she noticed, was pointing at her now, and the other two – freckled and blonde, both of them – were nodding.

"Excuse me," she said in her best icy voice as she moved to the fiction shelves.

"Ho, yes, cairtainly, Modom Custard," said the tall girl in the sheep-patterned jumper, and all three girls fell about laughing at the joke.

Tessa hardly noticed the titles of the books. She heard the girls move off to the door. Not one of them greeted Ned, she noticed. They clattered off down the steps and Tessa breathed a sigh of relief.

"I'm going back home," Dad said. "You two come back for lunch when you're ready. Right?"

Tessa knew the girls were still outside the van and she wished Dad hadn't spoken. His voice didn't sound right, too big and booming in the cramped van, too posh and southern amongst the local accents. She turned away from the shelves and moved quickly down the van.

"I'm ready," she announced, rather too brightly. Ned seemed oblivious to the gigglers; he just nodded over his open book.

Tessa followed Dad across the green, conscious of the three pairs of eyes scrutinizing them both: Dad's huge, shambling figure, with a mop of hair gathered in a pony-tail behind his cap; her leggy, slim one with its single long plait. She walked very tall and straight behind her father. Modom Custard, indeed! Tessa sniffed.

But inwardly she sighed. School was going to be a lot more difficult than she'd thought.

Chapter 4

The gigglers were all in her class, as were Jason Skilbeck and Ned, because there were only two junior classes in the little school. Ned nodded across to her, the girls smirked at her; only Jason spoke.

"It's Tessa Custard, Miss Marsden," he said. "I told you she'd be coming. Can she sit at our table?" Without waiting for an answer he waved Tessa over.

Miss Marsden, their teacher, smiled encouragingly. "Tessa *Gostard*, is it? Hello, Tessa. Would you like to join Jason's group?"

Even Tessa couldn't think of a way to refuse, and anyway there didn't seem to be any other spare places. The room was high and wide, with big church-like windows and a polished wooden floor, but it was very crowded. Tessa remembered the emptiness of the surrounding countryside. Where did they all come from? she wondered as she slid into her place.

Somebody made an explosive noise, like a sneeze gone wrong.

"Tracey Jones, don't start! I can't face it so early in the day," said Miss Marsden. And Tessa was surprised when Tracey, the girl in the sheepy sweater at the library van, promptly obeyed.

Everyone seemed to obey Miss Marsden. She didn't even raise her voice but whatever she wanted them to do, they got on and did it, Tessa noted. There was a set, ordered routine such as she'd not experienced in her busy, bustling city school. In spite of her misgivings, she found it rather soothing. Without speaking, she started on the comprehension test that Miss Marsden had given her.

She was so busy that she looked up in surprise when people began to clear up. She hadn't heard a bell, but it was obviously break time.

"I'll get you a tidy-box," said Jason importantly. He scuttled over to a store-room behind Miss Marsden's desk.

As Tessa waited for him to return she idly turned Jason's Maths book over. She was streets ahead of him, she was relieved to notice. She smiled and flipped back the cover, catching a glimpse of the name in the top right-hand corner of the book:

JASON SKILBECK, SUNNYSIDE, SLACK LANE, DELVER, DERBYS.

Her eyes lingered over the label, noting the way he printed the letter S, loose and sloppy like very thin, lazy snakes. It reminded her of something she'd seen recently – where was it?

"'Snot your book, that."

Tessa jumped at the sound of the voice.

Tracey Jones stood leaning over her. "Copying answers, are you?" she demanded.

Tessa looked across at her round, smug face, her round, pebble eyes, her round, pursed mouth. She wanted to hit her.

"No, I'm not," she said, coldly. "There's no point." Tessa meant that she was doing different work from Jason but Tracey thought she meant something else.

"Not good enough for you?" She leaned over Tessa's desk now, her pebbly eyes hard. "'Spect you'd rather have Noddy's book. He always gets everything right, he does."

Before Tessa could answer, Ned himself rushed past. He never even glanced in Tessa's direction and she flushed with annoyance – annoyance with Tracey Jones, with Ned Donovan, but most of all with herself for blushing.

Tracey watched him disappear along the corridor. "I expect you like him because he's a single-parent family like you." Tracey's eyes lit up with interest and Tessa knew she was ready to ask all sorts of awkward questions but luckily Jason reappeared, carrying a grey plastic tray.

"Here y'are, Tessa," he said. "Put your things in here then we can go out to play."

To play? It had been years since Tessa and her friends went out to play and she certainly did not want to play with Jason Skilbeck. But again she felt trapped.

To her surprise it was Tracey who rescued her. "Miss says we've got to show her round," she said to Jason.

"I can do that," said Jason, twitching at his bow tie importantly.

Tracey gave him a far from friendly push. "No you can't. Not the places we can show her," she said. "Come on, Tessa."

Tessa was quite pleased to be joining the girls, at last. She'd soon fill them in on things, impress them with tales of city life, take them over, get them organized.

The girls led her to the lavatory block across the playground. Tessa couldn't believe what she saw: a little red-brick building with half a dozen lavatory bowls squatted low behind green wooden doors which were without locks.

The three girls were watching her closely and Tessa felt that this was some kind of test, but she couldn't figure out the answer. If she showed how shocked she was at the little outdoor toilets, she'd be marked as a snob. On the other hand, if she passed on without comment, they'd never believe her tales of the luxuries at her city school.

"I'll hold your door if you want to go," Tracey encouraged her. And Tessa really did want to go.

"Thanks," she said, trying to sound carefree about the whole situation. Well, at least it was all beautifully clean, she thought, crouching over the little lavatory.

Suddenly the door was flung open and a whole crowd of faces peered in, shrieking,

"Red pants – Custard's got red pants!"

Tessa jumped off and hastily pulled her pants up. So that was the test!

Furiously, she flung herself through the door, scattering the audience, and rushed out into the playground. Her face was burning, tears stood in her eyes and her legs were trembling as she stalked off to the edge of the playground and glared across the common.

She was furious, not about the knickers; Tessa Gostard didn't care who knew the colour of her knickers, it was just the fact that those daft, giggly girls had caught her out with a mean, nasty trick.

"Did they get you, then?"

It was Jason, looking quite sympathetic. "Tracey Jones always tries that trick on anybody new," he said, striding out alongside Tessa and matching his step to hers. "We have indoor loos now – I'll show you. My dad's going to take them old 'uns down in the summer – he's a builder."

They walked across the playground past a wooden hut at the edge of the playing-field. There was a half-door over which Ned leaned, handing things out to a queue of infants.

Jason stopped. "Have you got some break?"

She shook her head, not understanding, not wanting to ask.

"I'll buy you some," he offered.

She followed his gaze over to Ned. He looked like a stranger now, leaning over the half-door, handing out crisps, sorting the change, too busy working, as usual, to notice her.

"He runs the tuck shop, does Noddy," explained Jason. "Miss always lets him 'cos he's good at maths. He's good at everything."

Jason sounded rather wistful. Tessa glanced down at him, standing twiddling his red bow tie. "Lucky him," she observed.

"D'you think so?" Jason sounded a bit relieved. "I never thought of Noddy being lucky. He's got no dad, only that Nora Donovan."

"What do you mean, 'that Nora Donovan'?

Nora's great," said Tessa vehemently. "And it's not his fault he has no dad."

Jason appeared to consider this remark. "It's hers, though," he said, mysteriously.

Tessa was longing to ask what he meant, but they'd arrived at the main entrance and Jason pointed along a corridor. "First left," he said, "and be quick, it's nearly time."

Time for what? thought Tessa. But as soon as she emerged from the new toilets, which had hot water, soap and paper towels, she saw the pupils coming back into school. She still hadn't heard a bell, but perhaps if you went to that school long enough you developed your own sense of time, like Jason had.

She had no time to ponder; Miss Marsden certainly knew how to keep her pupils busy. By the time the day was over, Tessa felt as if she'd done a whole week's Maths and English.

Ned was already at Nora's Place, mixing feeds, filling buckets with water. Without speaking, Tessa carried loads round to the various pens and cages. The field was growing well now so the donkeys, goats and geese were out to grass. Even so, Tessa noticed, Ned went round them all, patting and chatting. Tessa kept to the rabbits, which Ned found boring and she found nice and safe. As she poured the pellets into their bowls she remembered her first meeting with Jason Skilbeck – and then, the writing on his book.

"Have you ever seen Jason Skilbeck's writing?" she asked Ned after the feeding round.

Ned shook his head.

"Well, he makes the letter 'S' like this." With her finger she traced a long, thin 'S' in the dust on the floor.

Ned watched her. "Can't he use a pen?" he asked.

It was such a relief to have something to laugh about after that first day that Tessa fell about in an attack of giggles.

Ned grinned silently and waited for her to recover.

"No, look, where have you seen that sign before?" Tessa pointed to the mark in the dust.

Ned looked very carefully at it, then he stood up and examined it from several angles. At last he said, "On a spade?"

"Exactly!" Tessa looked at him, triumphantly.

"But Jason Skilbeck couldn't even lift it!" Ned pointed out. "He's a wimp and a weed and asthmatic as well!"

Tessa frowned. She'd been so sure that it was Jason's spade. "Well, his father's a builder; he'd

have a big shovel. And Jason might have painted their initial on it."

"One letter 'S' proves nothing," said Ned. He sat down and shuffled his back against the open door. He was thinking – Tessa could tell by the way he nodded and hummed to himself.

"We need proof," she said, quietly for once.

"Mmmm." Nod, nod, nod.

"We'll have to keep watch," she said, more loudly.

He nodded again, and again.

Then, "Badgerwatch!" They said it together.

By the time Tessa left, they'd agreed. Watching badgers would be a good cover for watching Skilbecks. Ned would draw up the plans, Tessa would organize the supporters.

"Because people're more likely to join if you ask them," said Ned.

"Me? But I'm a stranger here."

"That's sometimes an advantage." Ned spoke quietly but Tessa could hear the bitterness in his voice. "They'll come to you out of curiosity."

"About badgers?"

"About you – and your dad."

"Why should they be curious about us?"

"You're foreigners."

"We're not, we're English."

Ned studied her closely. "You don't look it," he said bluntly.

Tessa tugged at her plait and frowned. In the city no one even noticed the colouring she'd inherited from her mother: blue-black hair, brilliant dark eyes and coffee-coloured skin were quite common in the city, but were obviously exotic in Delver. Well, if it helped to get supporters for Ned's Badgerwatch, looking foreign would at least prove useful.

It was only when she ran up the lane that Tessa's enthusiasm waned. Where was she going to find any supporters in that village? In spite of Ned's theory, she was still a newcomer, a "grockle" they'd called her – and worse behind her back, she was sure.

"Hi, Tess – had a good day?" Dad called from the kitchen as she went in.

Tessa swallowed and tried to forget the names they'd called her. "Yeah," she assured her father. "It was OK. No hassle."

Her dad looked up quickly. "You'll have to give them time to get used to you, you know," he said.

"Like how long?"

"Oh, twenty years should do," he grinned. "Fish fingers all right for you?"

After tea they swopped news. Dad had

checked the badger sett again, but both spade and earth were undisturbed – as were the badgers, he believed; there were badger tracks around the sett. But whoever was after them hadn't been back – yet.

"I hope I've frightened them off just by being around," he said. "I really can't spend all my time up there."

So Tessa told him of the Badgerwatch plan – but not of her suspicions about Jason's handwriting.

"So how can we get enough people to watch the sett?" she asked. "We don't know anybody."

"Oh, I know a few people at work who'll be keen, and you know some at school."

"They won't do anything for me."

"Perhaps if Ned asks them?"

But according to Ned, that wouldn't work either; he seemed as much of an outsider as herself, thought Tessa. "It's no good," she wailed. "I haven't got any friends."

As if to contradict her somebody knocked loudly at the door.

"Well," said Dad. "Somebody's come to call – maybe a friend of yours." He turned and shouted down the passage. "We're in the kitchen – come right through."

And Jason Skilbeck came in.

"There you are," said Dad. "I'm sure Jason will be only too keen to join the Badgerwatch. Won't you, Jason?"

Chapter 5

"**P**ush off, Skilbeck!" Tessa was quite fed up
with Jason. He'd been round at Delves
Cottage every evening that week, and even at
school, he rarely left her alone. Turning her
back on him now, she held up Ned's poster,
pinned it on to the class notice-board and stood
back to admire the effect.

"'Snot level," said Jason. And he was right,
too. Ned's beautifully-drawn badgers looked
slightly drunk. Jason stepped up to the board
and adjusted the bottom edge of the poster.

"Vol-un-trees wanted," he read, slowly.

"Delves Wood Badgerwatch. Sign below if you're av . . . av . . ."

"Available," supplied Tessa. Handwriting wasn't Jason's only weak subject, she noted.

"Right," Jason agreed. He fished in his pocket, produced a slim, elegant ball-point pen and, sticking out his tongue in concentration, signed his name in the first space.

"*You* needn't sign," protested Tessa. "We know you're available."

"We?"

"Dad and Ned and Nora and me."

"Thought this was for kids."

Tessa sighed. "We need some adults as well – make it all official," she said.

Nora had pointed that out when she'd first heard about the Badgerwatch. Tessa had been indignant: this was Ned's project – and hers. But one evening, up in the woods, the two of them had met a couple of rough-looking older lads and their even rougher lurcher dogs. The lads had glared at Ned and whistled at Tessa and the dogs yapped and snarled. Tessa and Ned turned and ran all the way back to Delves Cottage with the jeers and laughter of the lads ringing through the trees. And they knew they'd certainly need help to face up to folk like that!

"We're hoping to get one adult for each session," she explained to Jason.

"I'm first on the list anyhow," said Jason. "I hope I'm in your dad's group. I'll know just what to do – I'm often up the woods, you know, 'cos my dad . . ." Jason's chatter stopped as if turned off. Tessa turned to look at him, puzzled at his abrupt silence. He flushed and offered her his pen. "'S your turn," he said.

She shook her head. "I'll sign after every-body else." She was afraid no one would sign if her name headed the list. Who'd want to join anything run by an incomer?

Jason shook his head and sniffed. "You ought to tell old Noddy to keep his name till last," he advised.

"Why? He's not new."

"Don't matter. Some folks'll never fit in, not in a thousand years," said Jason, sniffing repeatedly.

And Tessa had the feeling he was quoting somebody.

"Why not?" she challenged.

Jason produced a sparkling white hanky and blew his nose loudly. "Well, you know," he said. "What about his dad?"

Tessa was puzzled. "He doesn't seem to have one."

"There you are, then." Jason shoved the hanky, damp and squashed now, back into his pocket. "Never 'ad one, 'as he?"

Tessa had never heard Ned mention a father, but then Ned never mentioned anything much. And back where she came from, you never asked questions about people's parents; sometimes they had one, often two, and sometimes even three, like she used to have, when Granny Lila first came to live with them, before Mum left.

"Does it matter?" she asked, genuinely puzzled.

Jason shrugged. "Don't seem to matter to them, but folk talk, you know."

Tessa did know. She'd often imagined the things they were saying about Dad and herself, but that was because they were "incomers".

"Folk should mind their own business," she said tartly, glaring again at the poster. "What about your name?" she went on. "Will they join if they see that?"

Jason flushed. "They will if I tell 'em," he said. "You coming?"

Tessa reluctantly followed him out to the playground. She'd noticed that people often did do what Jason told them, provided he was generous with gifts from the tuck shop. Well, if they had to rely on Jason's bribes to get volunteers, it was going to cost him. Tessa grinned at the idea that Gary Skilbeck's money would be supporting Badgerwatch.

But in spite of Jason's proud boast that everyone would follow his example, and even though he bought generous helpings of "break" for anyone with an interest in badgers, there was no rush to sign the notice.

"Perhaps you should give us a talk about the badgers," Miss Marsden suggested, the following week. "Then people will understand what they're taking on."

Ned shook his head. "An expert," he said, "that's what we want."

"Your mum?" said Tessa.

There was a pause. Tessa felt she'd somehow put her foot in it, but she wasn't sure how.

Ned just stood, shaking his head.

Miss Marsden broke the silence, speaking brightly. "Would your dad be willing?" she asked Tessa. "After all, he works up there in the woods."

Another pause. Tessa knew very well that her dad would love to come and talk to the class; it was the kind of thing he was good at. So why was she hesitating? She daren't answer that, not even to herself. Miss Marsden and Ned were both looking at her.

"I'll ask him," Tessa muttered.

But when she got home Dad had news that drove everything else out of Tessa's mind. He was sitting at the kitchen table looking at some papers and maps. The kitchen was the one liveable room in the house now; the old wooden cupboards were stacked with tins and pots, a nearly-new washer was installed by the sink and a huge fridge-freezer muttered away by the door. Tessa loved coming home the back way, straight into the kitchen and over to the big wood-burning stove on which they cooked.

"Hi, Dads," Tessa said, rumpling the fuzzy hair on the top of his head. "What's for tea?"

Her dad looked up. "Is that the time?" he asked. "I've been so busy reading all this stuff. Why don't we just have a cup of tea and a sandwich? We can cook later."

Tessa grinned. "Cook later" in Dad's language

meant a tin of soup for supper. "OK," she said. "Cheese and pickle all right for you?"

As they made the sandwiches together, Dad told her the news. Gary Skilbeck had bought a few acres up in Delves Wood, just in the corner where the sett was. He was going to build holiday cottages there.

Tessa suddenly remembered Jason's odd silence when he'd signed up for the Badger-watch; he'd been going to brag about his dad but something stopped him. Did he know that his dad had bought the land?

"But they can't build right on top of a badger sett, can they?" she asked.

"He'll need planning permission," said Dad. "But he always seems to get that; he has contacts on the council."

They took their sandwiches over to the table and Dad opened up the map to show Tessa the corner of the woods which Gary Skilbeck now owned.

"There's the ruin of an old cottage there

still," he said. "Ned told me it was the original Delves Cottage two hundred years ago."

"But the badgers have a right to live there, haven't they?"

"Well," Dad sighed. "Gary Skilbeck must think he's got a right to build there. You see he's going to build on the old foundations and use the original materials so the new cottages will be within the conservation laws. They'll be a lot prettier than this red brick monstrosity."

"It's not a monstrosity, it's our house!" protested Tessa. Then she flushed as Dad grinned at her. Imagine her, defending the house she'd once hated so much! Well, it might be red brick, it might need a few coats of paint and hundreds of pounds' worth of repairs – there was even a leak in the roof; but she'd grown quite fond of the plain, four-square house set in a wilderness of garden. "I'd rather have our house than one of Skilbeck's monstrosities," she said. Then she had a thought. "What's he going to do about the badgers?"

He shook his head. "That's up to him. There are ways of leaving them undisturbed. It depends just where he builds and how far he's prepared to go to protect them."

Tessa remembered the big red face peering down at her from the Range Rover that morning, weeks ago. Gary Skilbeck didn't look like a badger-protector to her. "Are you going to see him?" she asked.

Dad shook his head. "It's not up to me," he said. "But it does mean the Badgerwatch has to get going quickly. Then at least we'll have some local interest; that might persuade our Mr Skilbeck to move a little carefully."

That reminded Tessa about the talk. "So can you come to school?" she asked. And will you get your hair cut? she wanted to add, but she knew it would be useless.

"I can pop in on Friday afternoon," Dad said. "But I'll need Ned's help – he knows far more about the woods than I do. Tell you what, we'll walk round there as soon as we've eaten, and

I'll have a chat with Ned. Work something out."

But they didn't find anyone up at Nora's Place; Ned and his mum had gone home by that time and Tessa suddenly realized she didn't even know where they lived.

Dad grinned. "Good job I hear a lot of village gossip at the pub," he said. "They live over the butcher's. Come on."

Tessa followed him slowly, reluctant to burst in on Nora and Ned when they hadn't been invited. At home in the city, she wouldn't have worried; her gang was always calling on each other and Dad was a well-known character in their flats. But Tessa felt they did things differently in the country. After all, nobody ever called to see them, except for Jason, and he didn't seem to be a typical villager.

"Dad!" she called, running to catch him up. "Do you think we should?"

"Should what?" He stood outside the butcher's, looking up at the windows above the shop.

"Call on them – when we haven't been invited."

He turned and looked at her, amazed. "Ned's a friend of yours, isn't he? And you know his mum?"

Tessa nodded anxiously. Dad never understood about privacy. His habit of running an open house back in the city had always caused problems with Mum. She'd wanted a home to themselves with a door firmly locked against most of Dad's friends, and Granny Lila allowed in by invitation only. She'd said she wanted her own space. Well, there was plenty of that in Canada.

But what if Nora liked *her* home to herself, too, *her* front door firmly locked, *her* own space? Tessa blushed at the idea of barging in on the Donovans.

"What's the matter with you, Tess?" Dad paused by a narrow yellow door down an alleyway by the shop. "You ashamed of me, or something?"

Tessa shook her head miserably and followed him. Her dad took her hand and pulled her up to him. "We've nothing to be ashamed of, you and me, Tess. People might think we don't belong here, and perhaps we don't – yet. But we're as good as any of them – Skilbecks, Donovans, anybody. D'you hear? And we're staying here so they'll have to get used to us. Right?" He squatted down and looked hard at her, shining blue eye to clouded brown one.

Tessa looked into his deeply tanned face and at his wild fuzz of hair. "OK, Dad," she said. And she tugged at his ponytail.

"OK, Tess, let's go!" He stood up and rang a bell set into the stone wall beside him.

When Ned answered the door, Tessa could see he wasn't pleased to see them. No nodding, no humming, he just stood there, hanging on to the door knob, looking up at her dad with his clear, cool gaze.

"Hi, Ned! I wonder if you have a moment?" Mr Gostard began. "Tess tells me I have to do a talk – about the badgers. I'd like to do it but I'll need your help."

Ned nodded now, up and down, up and down. "Mmmmmm," he hummed vaguely. Tessa was about to suggest that he should come over to Delves Cottage and talk to Dad another time when Nora called down the stairs.

"Who is it, Ned?"

"Tessa – and her dad."

"Well, bring them up then!"

It was an order. Ned turned and led the way up a narrow wooden staircase – no carpets, Tessa noticed – across a wide, empty landing, with a polished wooden floor, and into a long room with narrow windows all along one side.

Nora stood on a brilliant red rug flung diagonally across the wide, waxed floorboards.

"Hello, Mr Gostard," she held out a hand. "Nora Donovan."

"Hello, Nora." Tessa's dad bent his head to beam down at Nora. "Jim," he said simply. "Sorry to interrupt – I just wanted a word with

Ned – about the Badgerwatch. It seems they need someone to talk about it up at school."

Nora looked across at her son, and in the evening sunshine streaming through the windows Tessa noticed that she, too, looked pale and strained as she flopped back into a big, faded armchair and waved them to the sofa.

"Have you heard about the Skilbecks?" Tessa asked, importantly. She loved breaking news to people and this was the first time since coming to Delver that she'd had any.

Ned and Nora looked at her, amazed. "Well, yes, of course we've heard," said Nora, quite sharply. "How did you find out?"

"Planning Department," said Dad. "Man called up at the Forestry office today, showed me the exact area he's bought."

"Right on top of the badgers," Tessa burst in.

"Badgers?" Ned asked. "There are no badgers up at Nora's Place."

"Nora's Place?" Tessa and Dad spoke simultaneously.

Nora leaned forward. "I think we'd better start again," she said. "The lease for Top Field finishes in August and Gary Skilbeck won't renew it. We've got to be out by the first of August – animals and all."

"Any reason?" Jim Gostard spoke gently.

Nora looked across at Ned. Ned looked closely at the floor. "Well, we're not exactly popular in the village, what with the ramshackle sheds, noisy animals . . . and us." She shrugged.

There was a pause; even Tessa was silent. She was remembering what Jason had called Ned's mother: "*that* Nora Donovan". He'd sounded just like Granny Lila when she mentioned a troublesome neighbour. Was Nora troublesome? How? Tessa felt she dare not ask.

"Go on." Ned nodded across to his mother. "They're OK." Tessa felt a surge of pride at this rather grudging praise.

Nora took a deep breath. "Well, you can't entirely blame them, I suppose. Not only did they get a female part-time vet, but they got one with a child and no husband – and no premises!"

There was silence. Nora looked into the distance and Ned sat quite still and silent, examining the floorboards closely.

"So what's Skilbeck going to do with the field?" Jim Gostard spoke briskly, before Tessa could start asking awkward questions.

"I imagine he wants to build on it," said Nora.

"And up in the woods, too," said Dad.

"Right on top of the badgers," Tessa said again.

Nora smiled. "Ah, I see now. He's going to rebuild the old forester's cottage, I suppose."

Ned nodded, sadly. "Not much point in Badgerwatch now," he said. "Soon be no badgers to watch."

"And no Nora's Place either," added Tessa. "No goats to feed, no geese to round up, no rabbits or donkeys." Even the thought of losing the dreaded donkeys made her feel tearful just then.

"Oh, come on! Don't be so defeatist!" Jim Gostard glared round at them. "It's even more important to keep watch now," he said. "On the badgers, on Nora's Place – and on Gary Skilbeck." He stood up straight, almost cracking his head on the cruck beam which supported the old roof. "And we'll start the campaign up at the school on Friday. Right, Ned?"

Tessa groaned inwardly. A campaign, she thought. I hoped he'd left all that behind in the city. She looked at Ned. He nodded over to Dad and they grinned at each other.

"Now, this is what we do," said Tessa's dad.

Chapter 6

So Dad and Ned threw themselves into drawing up the plans for the Badgerwatch scheme. They made maps, wrote letters and drew up a rota of volunteers – mainly themselves and a few adults from the County Badgerwatch Scheme.

Tessa had been proud to be one of the first Badgerwatchers. The idea seemed so exciting. The reality was utterly boring. They sat in silence in the bracken, getting damper and colder as night came on, and not one badger put in an appearance. After what seemed like a whole night to Tessa, though it was only about an hour, they gave up. Tessa was not so quick to volunteer after that; she found herself plenty to do at Nora's Place. The real animals at Nora's Place were so much more appealing than invisible badgers.

"You're better than badgers, any time," she told the little orphan lamb that nuzzled up to her, sucking at her fingers, in the barn one afternoon. "Are you hungry, little Lambo?" she asked. "I'll make you a feed as soon as Nora gets back with the van."

"Still talking to them animals," observed Jason Skilbeck, peering over the stable door.

The first thing Tessa noticed was his missing bow tie; then how flushed and sweaty he was – almost scruffy. "What are you doing here?" she asked in a far from friendly voice.

"Looking for Nora."

"Well, you won't find her here; the van's out."

"What about Noddy?"

Tessa glared. "Ned", she said firmly, "is working with my dad." She pushed the lambs away and stood leaning over the stable door.

"What's up with you?" she asked Jason. Obviously something was: his pale blue denim jacket looked as if he'd dragged it through a hedge and the knees of his jeans were muddy green.

He hesitated as if trying to remember a message. "There's a dog up in the woods," he said. "It's been hurt."

"How?"

He looked at her blankly, then blinked rapidly. "I don't know, do I?" he asked fiercely. "I only know it's in a rare old mess." His chin wobbled and he sniffed hard.

He was trembling, Tessa noticed. "Is it your dog?" she asked, a little more sympathetically. After all, any hurt dog deserved to be helped, even Jason's.

"No," he said very sharply. "It's not mine."

"Well, go and ring the vet's surgery in

Jessup." Tessa knew that if the animal was badly injured, Nora would pass it on to the surgery anyway; her van was only a sort of first-aid post.

Again he shook his head. "No, they'll not be in, this time of day."

Tessa was puzzled. "But they all have car-phones, don't they?"

"Oh . . . don't argue, Tessa Custard. Argue, argue, argue, it's all you ever do!" Jason said vehemently.

Tessa opened her mouth to argue some more but was stopped by the noise of the van turning into the field. Jason shot off and Tessa followed, quickly overtaking him on the slope and waving to Nora to stay down by the gate. By the time Jason puffed up to join them, Nora had heard the problem and was ready for off.

"Hop in, both of you," she said. "Sounds as if we need to hurry."

She drove round what she called the "top road" to the woods and parked the van in a little pulling-in place. Jason set off down the woods almost before Nora had locked the van. "This way," he was calling.

Nora and Tessa followed him down the track, then through the undergrowth until they came to a bank with a bit of old wall on top.

Who'd build a wall in the middle of the woods? Tessa wondered.

Nora was already on her knees, and Tessa moved towards her, to see what she was doing. Then she stepped back, her eyes squeezed tight, her stomach heaving.

Propped up against the bank was a small white dog. At least, Tessa supposed, it had been white. Now it was smeared with mud and blood. Its eyes were opened but glazed over and at the side of its neck was a deep gash, oozing with blood and covered with flies.

Nora had already removed her sweat shirt and wrapped it round the little animal. The dog snarled at her feebly and lifted its lip but it was too weak to protest.

"Come on, my lovely." Nora spoke gently as she picked up the dog and set off back to the van. Jason walked with her but Tessa stood for a moment, looking round. There was something familiar about those trees over the wall, something that reminded her . . . She ran up the bank and peered over the top. Down below she saw the hollow where she had fallen down that first day in the woods with Ned. The hollow where they'd found the spade; where the badgers lived.

She looked very closely for signs of the spade but it had gone. The earth was all churned up, as if freshly disturbed, though whether by badgers or by humans, Tessa couldn't tell. She ran swiftly through the undergrowth and caught up with the others on the track.

"Was the dog on that bank when you found him?" she asked Jason.

He just nodded slightly as he puffed his way up the track. Nora looked puzzled. "He's very damp and muddy," she said. "Yet there are no burrows in that bank."

"Must 'ave been rabbiting," puffed Jason.

Nora soothed and patted the bundle in her arms. "Poor lad, he's probably been stuck somewhere, then got himself out only to be attacked by another animal."

"Another dog?" asked Tessa.

Nora shook her head and paused for a moment; the dog was only small but he was almost unconscious and quite a dead weight. "I'll know better when I get him cleaned up."

Back in the van Nora got everyone organized. "Kettle on," she said to Tessa. "Mix me some hot water and disinfectant in a clean bowl from the cupboard. Cotton wool and a clean towel – in the drawer by the sink." She laid the little dog down on a plastic sheet on the work-top. Tessa was reminded of the first day she'd seen the camper van; the day she'd stood awkwardly aside listening to Ned bossing her. She smiled to herself as she smoothly went about her tasks.

She felt very important. This time it was Jason who hung about awkwardly.

"Lucky you found him," she said.

He nodded, but he didn't look pleased with himself as he so often did at school. He didn't even look at the dog he'd rescued, just kept looking down into the woods, as if watching for someone.

Before Tessa could ask who he was looking for, the kettle boiled and she poured water and antiseptic into a metal bowl. The little animal whimpered and even half-growled as Nora cleaned the raw flesh along its neck, murmuring softly to him all the time she worked. Tessa watched the short, strong hands moving gently over the wounds and silently handed her chunks of cotton wool.

Eventually Nora stood back. "He'll do for now," she said. "But he ought to go to the surgery."

"Can't we drive him there?" suggested Tessa.

Nora turned to Jason. "Any idea whose dog

this is?" she asked. "Any farmer with a good terrier like this would happily pay for surgery."

Jason shook his head without even looking at the dog.

Nora sighed. "They're deep gashes," she said. "But I'll have a go. Come on, Jason, hold his head while I put on a dressing."

"No!" Jason backed off down the step. "I got to get back – me mum's expecting me . . . it's me tea-time . . ." And once on the road he turned and ran.

Nora grinned. "Can't take it, some people," she said. "Blood," she explained to Tessa.

But Tessa wasn't so sure it was blood that frightened Jason off. At school somebody was always falling down, grazing a knee or cutting a finger, and you could tell those who didn't like to see. Ned, for one, in spite of his interest in animals, could never bear to watch a pupil in pain or discomfort. But Jason revelled in it; he loved to fuss about, run and fetch Miss, offer one of his immaculate hankies and a lot of advice. Whenever there was an accident, Jason was there. So why had he run off just now? What *was* he afraid of?

"Well, you'll have to hold him; I must pull the edges of the cuts together before I dress them." Nora's voice broke through Tessa's thoughts and for some time she was too busy holding on to the animal's neck and her own queasy stomach to think about Jason.

When they'd finished they laid the dog on one of the passenger seats behind the driver. Tessa sat alongside him to make sure he didn't slip around and Nora drove down to Delves Cottage.

"Do you think you can keep him for a day or two?" she asked Tessa. "He needs to be kept warm and I can't take him home with me; our kittens will give him no peace."

Tessa was alarmed. She knew her dad had very firm ideas about pets; he'd fought a long battle to clean up the city parks and only just tolerated Granny Lila's cat. Plants, yes, he had lots of those on every window-sill and out on the balcony, shrubs and climbers in pots, even little seedlings that were baby trees, but never an animal.

"You'll have to ask Dad," she said.

"Of course," Nora nodded easily. "But before we ask we'll take him in." She leaned into the van and lifted the bandaged dog out. "Come on, little beauty," she murmured. "Home and safe now."

Ned was already at the door when they started along the path. "It's all right," he said, assuming his mother had come to fetch him. "I've got my bike." Then he saw what she was carrying.

"Shhh," said Nora as she eased into the cottage with her burden. "Hi, Jim!" Tessa heard the rather false cheeriness in her voice. "Could you do me a favour?"

Tessa and Ned grinned at each other and moved into the kitchen.

The terrier was already looking round, wild-eyed, snapping feebly at anything that came within reach. "Could do with a drop of milk, I expect – you wouldn't have any brandy, would you?" Nora asked Dad.

"Only cheap Spanish." He grinned. "But I don't know . . ."

"Just a few days – till I get rid of those kittens," Nora promised.

"Why not leave him in the stables?"

"Well . . . nights are cool still and he's in shock. Anyway, those stables are nothing but sheds and the donkeys quite fill them."

Tessa's dad looked at the little body laid out on the table. "I don't know," he said again. "I never had an animal before."

"You'll be all right with him. I'll send over supplies – I'll need to see him every day for a while anyway. And somebody might come forward to claim him quite soon. Now, have you got a box?"

"Has the Queen got jewels?" Dad went out the back and brought in one of their packing boxes. He put it up on the table and cut down one side. Then Tessa brought some old dust-sheets and a piece of towelling to put on top. Gently, Nora laid the dog in the box. "There, my lovely, you'll be fine."

Ned poured the last of the milk into a saucer and held it close so that the dog could lap at it without too much pain. He didn't growl at Ned, just sniffed at his hand then fell back, exhausted. He obviously wanted to sleep but his neck was too painful when he put his head down. Dad swept one of Grandma Lila's patchwork

cushions from a chair and tucked it under the dog's head.

"I hope you're not going to tell me he needs milk every hour through the night," he said.

Nora beamed. "Not every hour," she said. "But if you can get him to take to a little more before you go to bed, and if you should be around during the night . . ."

Dad groaned.

"I'll feed him at night, Dad," said Tessa.

"She can, Jim," said Ned. "She's good with animals." Tessa, taken by surprise at Ned's praise, flushed and gazed at her father with bright, pleading eyes.

Dad looked across the table at Tessa. "OK, but don't get too involved," he warned. "It's not our dog. We might find he's already reported missing."

"I doubt it," said Nora grimly. "It's the owner who's missing." And they sat round the kitchen, keeping watch over the sleeping animal while Tessa recounted how they'd found him.

"So how did Jason come to be up in the woods?" wondered Dad. "He told me his mother never allowed him there."

Nora smiled. "She wouldn't allow him out at all if he didn't have to go to school," she said. "Poor old Jason."

"Huh!" Ned almost choked into his Coke.

"Shush, Ned. Just because we don't like his father doesn't mean to say we can't sympathize with the boy. The trouble with Jason is that his dad wants to turn him into a right Rambo and his mum wants to keep him as Christopher Robin. Between the two of them they must make his little life a misery."

Tessa was thoughtful. Nora was right; Jason was a mixture of bossy bravado and mummy's boy. "So why was he up in the woods?" she asked. "It was right above that place where we found the spade," she told Ned. "But it's gone now."

Ned looked shocked. "They've been back." His face tightened with misery.

"Yes," Tessa agreed. "I saw fresh earth all dug over. And Jason was acting very oddly."

"He always is," muttered Ned.

"No, oddly even for him." Tessa was enjoying herself now; she liked an audience and she'd not had one since leaving her old friends. "I think he knows whose dog it is and he's under orders not to tell."

"Under orders? Come on, Tess, you've been reading too many *Famous Fives*." Dad was teasing but Tessa knew he was serious. "You can't go accusing Jason of being involved in something you know nothing about."

"But Dad, we have all the evidence . . ."

"You have nothing. Now you just stop clacking that tongue of yours. D'you hear me? Promise, now!"

Tessa nodded crossly. She could tell, by the twang of Granny Lila in his voice, that her father was worried. "So what are you going to do?" she challenged him.

"Watch and wait," said her dad. "I'm keeping

a careful eye on that path; the badgers were still around this morning so nobody's harmed them . . . unless . . ."

"Unless . . ." Ned echoed. They both looked over to the dog.

"What sort of wounds were they?" Dad asked Nora.

"Scratches, deep, quite vicious; might have killed a less wiry dog . . ."

"Badgers." Ned said the word softly. "That dog's been sent down after badgers." His face was quite white, his eyes glinted with tears.

"And his owners were disturbed so they upped and left him." Dad's voice was gentle but Tessa could hear the cold anger in it.

They all looked again at the little white terrier, sleeping uneasily, legs atwitch, back shuddering now and then.

"Poor little devil," said Nora. "No wonder he's in shock."

"No wonder Jason was, too," said Tessa. "He knows more than he's saying."

"Well, he did rescue the dog," smiled Nora. "That's the most important thing. Come on, Ned, we'd better get back and report this nasty incident to the police. We can leave the dog to Tessa; I'm sure he'll respond to her."

Dad stood at the gate and waved them off but Tessa sat watching the twitching, panting little dog, checking her bits of evidence. What if somebody else had been clearing out the badgers and Jason had disturbed them? What if they'd run off leaving the terrier behind? Why didn't Jason say? Was it because he was afraid? Or was he protecting somebody? Somebody he knew well, somebody who wanted to get rid of the badgers? Like Gary Skilbeck, his dad?

I'll talk to him at school, she thought. If I chat to him, he might let something out. But then she remembered her promise to Dad: "Stop clacking that tongue of yours," he'd said.

Oh, I will, she promised again, but not too hard.

Chapter 7

Secretly, when they were on their own, Tessa called the dog Custard. He wasn't supposed to have a name, in case anyone came to claim him. But she couldn't go on calling him "the dog" and she'd soon hit on the idea of passing her hated nickname on to him; if anyone in the family had to be Custard it might as well be him.

"'Bye, Custard," she whispered before she left for school on the morning of Dad's talk. "You just rest now and get better."

Delves Lane was wet and shiny after an early

downpour. Tessa stepped carefully round the puddles and skirted the grass verges; she should have worn her wellies but they were still muddy from last night's walk up to the badger sett. And a right waste of time that had turned out to be – again! I hope talking about badgers is more interesting than watching them, thought Tessa, otherwise we'll never get anyone interested in joining Badgerwatch.

She jumped the last puddle as the white Range Rover swished past, hooting loudly and spraying her with muddy water.

"You were on the wrong side of the road again!" Gary Skilbeck leaned out of the window.

Tessa looked down at her jeans and then glared up at the car. "I was only trying to keep my feet dry," she explained, coldly.

Mr Skilbeck had the grace to look embarrassed. "Here." He dangled an extremely white handkerchief out of his window. "Mop yourself on that."

Tessa took it and dabbed at the damp patches

around her knees. She stopped when she noticed the handkerchief turning brown with mud stains.

"It's all right," Mr Skilbeck told her. "Just pass it back to Jason at school; his mum'll get the stains out." Waving back at her, he pulled away.

That was quite kind, thought Tessa, mopping more vigorously now. But then she remembered Nora's face, that evening when she'd told them about losing the field. And she remembered her Custard and how somebody – possibly Gary Skilbeck – had left him to die in the badger sett. No, she decided, Gary Skilbeck was not kind at all.

But he'd done more than help her dry her jeans: he helped her to corner Jason. Normally, it would have been easy to have a chat with Jason at school; he'd rather chat than work any day. But that morning he didn't even sit down next to Tessa. He flitted to and fro, cleaning the gerbils, watering plants, taking an extra turn at the computer, joining the measuring group for Maths. It was as though he'd read Tessa's mind and knew what she was planning.

By dinner time she was feeling desperate. There'd be no opportunity to talk to him that afternoon; Dad and Ned were planning a full programme of badger talk. Pushing her lemon meringue pie aside, Tessa wandered outside to ponder the problem.

It always surprised her that there were no fences round the school area of the green; everyone stayed inside some invisible fence, within earshot of the dinner ladies. Unlike her old school, Delver Primary had no high wall, no locked gate, and yet nobody seemed to want to escape. Even those pupils who went home to dinner, like Jason Skilbeck, just drifted back across the common and joined in the games as early as they could.

Like Jason Skilbeck! Tessa smiled; now she knew where she'd catch him. Looking cautiously around, she took a couple of steps outside the non-existent boundary. The dinner lady was across on the asphalt, organizing a hopscotch competition, and nobody noticed Tessa. One advantage of having no friends, she thought as she scuttled along the edge of the common to the little bus shelter.

Settling herself on a corner of the shiny bench, Tessa looked around with interest. There was only one bus, later in the afternoon, so she'd be undisturbed. The little shelter was built of the same grey stone as most of the village houses, with a blue slate roof, just like a little house itself. Inside it was always swept clean and the bench seemed to be polished. By all those fat country bums, Tessa giggled to herself. She slid along the smooth bench and peeped out across the green.

Giggles turned to a broad grin as she saw Jason puffing up the hill. Tessa pulled back and squashed herself into a corner. She kept quite still until Jason had almost passed the shelter, without glancing in.

"Jason!" she called gently, in a voice quite unlike her own.

He turned and panic flooded his eyes. But before he could run, Tessa was towering over him, gripping his arm and steering him into the shelter. She was a strong girl, tall and wiry, like her dad.

"Whatcher doing then?" Jason blustered. "You're not allowed this far out, you're a dinner girl."

"Nobody's noticed," Tessa assured him. "Except you, and you're not going to tell, are you?" She tightened her grip on his arm.

"Ow! 'Course not," he said hastily. "I'm your mate, aren't I?"

"Are you?" Tessa narrowed her eyes like the television detectives did when they were interrogating criminals. "You haven't asked how Cus— that little dog is," she accused him.

"How is he?" Jason said, obediently.

"Very weak, but holding on. He lost a lot of blood, you know."

Jason began to sneeze violently, persistently. "Hay fever," he gasped. "I shouldn't be sitting out here."

Tessa ignored that. "You know how the dog got hurt, don't you?"

"Yeah – it was fighting."

"But what was it fighting? You know that too, don't you?"

If she'd thought to frighten Jason, Tessa was mistaken. He was too taken up with his own suffering to think about the dog. With his free hand he took out a large white handkerchief, shook it and blew his nose several times. Tessa waited, but Jason wasn't talking. She watched his performance with the handkerchief, mopping his eyes, sniffing a great deal, and she suddenly had an idea.

"I've got your dad's hankie here." Catch him off guard, she thought, he might let something out.

"My dad?" And certainly he looked a bit worried now.

"Yeah – he lent it to me when he splashed puddles all over me down the lane this morning." Tessa produced the handkerchief, stained and rumpled after a morning in her back pocket. "He said to give it back to you," she told him.

Jason looked down his dripping nose at it. "I'm not taking that back home," he said. "She'll only throw it out."

"Throw it out?" Tessa was horrified at the thought of such waste. "Why?" And as soon as she asked she thought she knew the answer.

Not entirely, though.

"It's not just you being strangers and all," Jason shrugged. "It's germs. She can't stand 'em. Scrubs and rubs and hoovers all day, just to keep 'em out."

And Tessa realized why Jason was always so impeccable. Every day another shirt, pair of socks, shining shoes and, of course, the spotless, well-ironed white hanky. She thought of the bits of loo paper Dad and she used for hankies, of Dad's shirt and cords in the wash once a week, of her knickers floating in the bath with her. And she envied Jason Skilbeck.

"It must be nice to have a mum to clean up after you and to live in a posh house like yours," she said, forgetting the interrogation and loosening her grip on his arm.

"Must be nice to do what you like and have nobody moaning on at you," said Jason. "Haven't you got a mum, then?"

"Yes I have," Tessa said, sharply. "But she doesn't moan on at me."

"Well, she can't, can she, if she's not here?" Jason pointed out. "Run away, has she?"

"No she has not." Tessa didn't like the way this was turning out. She'd never discussed her mother's departure with anyone, not even Granny Lila. And here was this sniffly lad, getting her to admit to thoughts she'd shut away a year ago. "She's working abroad." It sounded better than admitting her mother had gone back home to Canada. It was abroad, and she really was hoping to get a job out there.

But Jason seemed to have lost interest in Tessa's mum.

"Going away myself soon," he said.

"On a holiday?" Now they were back on the right track, Tessa thought. If the Skilbecks were going off for a week or two, it would leave the place clear for the Badgerwatch and give Nora time to find a new place for the animals.

"Boarding school," said Jason gloomily, and he sneezed several times. "I want to go up to the Manor Comp with you lot, but Mum thinks you're all too rough and Dad thinks you're all too soft. He says boarding school will toughen me up." And he sniffed miserably into his hanky.

Tessa grinned at the thought of Jason being toughened up. "Jolly japes in the Upper Fourth," she grinned. "What ho, Skilbeck Minor!" And she was so taken with her own wit and Jason's apparent wimpishness that she forgot to keep hold of his arm.

Jason, not entirely the wimp, jumped up and was off down the path while Tessa was still laughing at her own joke.

"You'll be late back," he called. "They've gone in!"

Friday afternoon was always special for pupils at Delver Primary: "activities", it was called. The two top classes were combined and the pupils could choose which activity they wanted to do, changing every half-term. When she'd first arrived, Tessa had no idea what to choose; the only "activity" she'd done in the city was her cycling proficiency and basketball. But there was no team at Delver and she'd passed her cycling certificate, so she'd joined the bird watchers, as a sort of thank you to the mallards.

But this Friday was special; all the groups were to meet together for the Badgerwatch talk. Tessa had already heard grumbles about this from people who wanted to get on with their fabric printing or their fantasy games, and she felt rather embarrassed about the whole thing. But Miss Marsden had insisted that this was a community project and they'd all meet together.

So, after registration, they pushed all the tables back and set out the chairs in front, whilst Ned trundled in the television trolley and set up the video. Tessa began to worry about Dad now; they'd never had a video at home and he was famous for breaking things. And even if he managed to run the video, he'd still sound "foreign" to Tracey Jones and her gigglers. She had already started to sound more like the rest of the class, broadening her vowels and adding "like" to every other sentence, but she hadn't dared to suggest that to her dad. He'd come on like a character from *EastEnders* and they'd all laugh at him. Tessa sat in the middle of the chattering group, feeling hot, her tummy aching, dreading the moment when Dad would appear.

She didn't even need to look; there was a

sudden hush as Ned pulled out a display screen filled with posters – and Dad was pushing the other end. Tessa screwed her tummy muscles tightly to stop the butterflies twitching, and closed her eyes. She knew that the other fifty pairs would be watching her dad, not one of them missing the mass of wiry hair, the dreaded ponytail and the earring glinting amongst it all. And for a moment she felt a twinge of sympathy for Jason; after all, he was no more responsible for his father's building plans than she was for her father's long hair.

Feeling a hard nudge in her ribs, she thought Jason had come to sit by her, but when she opened her eyes she saw it was Tracey Jones.

"Wake up, Custard. Don't you want to listen to your dad?" she whispered loudly, and her band of gigglers sniggered.

Before Tessa could even think of a cutting reply, her dad was speaking.

"Hi!" He greeted the pupils with a raised hand. "Jim Gostard."

No one spoke. Tessa felt herself going hot all over, embarrassed by her father's casual manner, furious with the other pupils. But just when she felt she could stand it no longer, Ned raised a hand and called, "Hi, Jim!"

Everyone laughed and the tension was broken. Miss Marsden perched on a table, to keep an eye on everyone, Ned ambled back to his seat and Tessa's dad started talking.

Or rather, he started by listening. He asked them to tell him all they knew about the woodlands around Delver, the old stories, the fruits and flowers they collected, the animals and birds they'd seen. He listened to everyone in turn and then told them about his work in the city parks, planting new trees, protecting old ones, and about the Canadian forests where he'd worked as a young man.

No one stirred, no one fidgeted or whispered; he seemed to have them hypnotized by his deep, soft voice, his tanned face and wide, white smile. He told them about the trees, the patterns of life they formed, the habitats they provided for birds, insects, animals – badgers.

Then Ned started the video and everyone shuffled round a bit to see the screen. Tessa was vaguely surprised that Jason hadn't pushed to the front; he usually did at television time. Perhaps, like her, he was even a bit fed up with the badgers; it seemed to her that they'd taken all Ned's attention from the problems with Nora's Place.

But watching the film was easier than watching for badgers in the woods. Tessa was soon entranced; left to themselves, badgers had a really good life, it seemed. Snug underneath the ground all day in their clean and comfortable sett, out to play and hunt every night with the family, mum and a dad badger ever-ready to protect the cubs. Well – protect them and train them too! Tessa smiled at the shot of the mother taking a wide swipe at a wandering cub. Over-protective, like Jason's mum, she thought. She looked round to share the joke with him, but the curtains were drawn against the sun and she couldn't see him in the gloom.

Tessa turned her attention to the film once more and was soon caught up in a project to construct an artificial observation hide. That's the way to badgerwatch, she thought; the animals have a safe run and the humans can watch in comfort.

After the film it was question time. All the pupils fired the questions they'd prepared at Mr Gostard, who sometimes had to pass them on to Ned. Tessa didn't ask anything; she just sat there feeling relieved it had all gone well. And although she was pleased that her dad was so popular now, it was Ned who amazed her, speaking so fluently, answering so confidently. If only Nora could have heard him, Tessa thought, she'd be so proud.

But now there was a pause as the pupils looked down their lists and Miss Marsden stood up ready to start her thank-you speech. Then Tracey Jones piped up.

"Is it true that they're going to build some houses up in Delves Wood and won't that scare the badgers away and my mum says we need more houses and people are more important than badgers . . ." She finished with a gush of giggles and looked round as if for applause.

"Well, your mum's right," said Jim Gostard. And he smiled, his brilliant, wide smile, looking straight at Tracey, who blushed and simpered. "People are important and they do need houses, but there are ways of leaving the badgers undisturbed . . ." He went on to tell them how badgers and humans could live alongside each other so long as the humans built carefully and respected the badgers' habits.

But Ned would have none of this. He stood up and almost shouted. "Badgers have been nearly wiped out in this country because of building or cruel humans who gas and even send fierce dogs down after them." And he glared all round accusingly, at Jason, thought Tessa, following his gaze, but she couldn't actually spot Jason just then.

Miss Marsden, anxious to smooth things over, started on her speech of thanks. Everybody clapped, Ned rushed round giving out leaflets about the Badgerwatch and several girls rushed forward to greet Tessa's dad as if he were a pop star.

But Jason Skilbeck was nowhere to be seen.

Chapter 8

" 'Ave you got our Jason 'ere?"

Gary Skilbeck's round pink face peered over the gate at Delves Cottage. He sounded very angry. Tessa looked up from the wilderness that was the front garden and shook her head.

Nobody had noticed he was missing at the end of school. Nobody except Tessa. She'd said nothing, partly because she felt she "owed him one" for not telling on her dinnertime escape. In any case, they were all too busy clearing up the classroom and chattering about badgers to notice he wasn't there.

Then the younger children drifted in, looking for their brothers and sisters, and suddenly the classroom had emptied. Dad swept Ned and Tessa out to the van and Nora invited them to come back to supper later on, to celebrate the launch of the Badgerwatch.

So now, Tessa was scrabbling through the wilderness trying to put together a bunch of flowers for Dad to take to Nora. She had a vision of Dad, bowing low over Nora's little white hand, presenting her with masses of red roses, like in the adverts on TV. Trouble was, the roses were lost in the brambles and even Tessa had to admit that Nora's hands were neither tiny nor ultra-white. And as if that wasn't enough to worry about, she now had to face this angry man at the gate.

Mr Skilbeck leaned over and peered round the bushes as if Jason was hiding from him. "He's always round here after school, his mam tells me."

He probably was, thought Tessa. But she

never saw him because she always stayed up at Nora's Place after school until Dad came to collect her. She was about to explain all this when Dad's voice drifted down from the bedroom.

"Tess – have I got a clean shirt?" Two pairs of eyes looked up, Gary Skilbeck's blue and sharp with anxiety, Tessa's dark and clouded. "I'll be right down," said Dad. And he was.

"Hello, it's Mr Skilbeck, isn't it?" He was down the path in three giant strides, his fuzzy damp hair streaming behind him. "Come in, man, come in."

But Gary Skilbeck stood still. "The wife's waiting for me," he said. "In quite a state. Our Jason's not been home for his tea. We know he hangs around here quite a bit . . ."

There was accusation in his voice now. Tessa, glaring over the gate, came and stood in front of her dad, as if to shield him.

Dad spoke gently. "Yes, Jason does sometimes call here, but he always goes home in time for tea. He hasn't been today at all, has he, Tess?"

Tessa shook her head and chewed her lip. She had a sudden picture of Jason running away from the bus-shelter that afternoon. To get away from her, she'd assumed, and go into school through the infants' entrance. But had he? Tessa said nothing.

"You sure he hasn't called here?" Mr Skilbeck indicated the garden. "You could have missed him in this lot."

"But if he'd called to see us, why would he hide in the garden?" said Dad.

Mr Skilbeck sighed. "I dunno," he said, and for a moment Tessa felt almost sorry for him, but he went on. "When I find the little devil he'll have some explaining to do, I can tell you." And he scowled at Jim Gostard, as if waiting for him to do a bit of explaining.

"Well, if he does call here in the next half hour or so, I'll bring him straight home myself," Tessa's dad promised. "Right?"

Mr Skilbeck nodded. "Just as long as you know." And still there was that threat in his voice.

Threat of what? Tessa watched Mr Skilbeck clamber into the Range Rover. She screwed her hand round in her pocket and found the stained hanky. She did wish she'd told somebody about Jason's disappearance.

"Get a move on, Tess, Nora's expecting us at six." Dad rushed back up the path. Too late to say anything now, thought Tess, following him and unfastening her hair as she went.

They had a lovely supper; everything was home-grown and home-made. Tessa wasn't too sure about the fresh trout, until Ned showed her how to take it clean off the bones, then she loved its earthy taste, and soft, buttery texture. After that they had roast chicken that tasted nothing like the American fried chicken she ate back in the city.

"Free-range – from one of the farms up on Debdale," Nora explained. And she told Dad about all the good food you could buy, if you knew where to call. "You'll soon have a freezer full of poultry and fish and game, and the fruit season's right on us. Then if you top up with bread and stuff on market day, you'll never be without a meal."

She smiled encouragingly at Jim, pushing up her huge red glasses as she spoke. Nora was wearing lipstick, Tessa noticed, and a big red shirt over black jeans. Tessa liked the way she dressed, without fuss, but smart enough for you to see she'd bothered.

She herself had brushed her hair and left it hanging loose about her shoulders just to show it was an important occasion; she'd even ironed the patchwork skirt Granny Lila had made for her. And Dad looked magnificent in his one and only clean white shirt with his very nearly clean black cords.

Only Ned looked the same, but he always did. Neat and tidy in his checked shirt and jeans, he brought in the pudding he'd made: an amazing concoction of bread and red berries all soaked in juice and topped with cream.

"Summer pudding – he's been clearing out last summer's fruit from the freezer," said Nora. "Ned's a much better cook than I am. We pick all our berries at that fruit farm the other side of the woods."

The mention of Delves Wood took them back to the afternoon's triumphs. Ned and Dad enjoyed telling Nora all about their talk but Tessa was unusually silent. She was thinking about Jason, surprised to find how worried she was; usually she was irritated by him, but now, for some reason, she felt guilty. Tessa pushed back her plate and sighed. Well, perhaps he'd been home for his tea by now, she thought. And she hoped he hadn't got too much hassle from his dad.

They were helping Nora to clear the table and Ned was grinding coffee beans when there was a banging at the door downstairs.

"Who on earth can that be?" asked Nora.

"I'll bet somebody's got a sick budgie or something. They always come to the door when . . ."

She rushed downstairs, opened the door and stopped. Tessa, peering from the landing, saw a small, fair woman, dressed as if she was on her way to some other, posher party. Tessa saw silvery highlights in her newly-set hair and shiny red nails tipping white, clenched fingers. A faint, lingering scent drifted up the stairs. Mum, thought Tessa. But the memory disintegrated as soon as the woman spoke.

"Errum . . . ahm sorry to disterb you . . . I rang th' bell but . . ." Broad Derbyshire.

"We can't always hear it in the kitchen." Nora sounded as dazed as Tess felt. "Well, you'd better come up, Mrs Skilbeck."

Tessa hastily backed away into the shadows on the landing.

"Come into the sitting room," she heard Nora say. "If it's a sick animal, I'm afraid . . ." She almost pushed the woman in front of her.

At the top of the stairs, Mrs Skilbeck looked round, rather wildly.

"It's not an animal," she muttered. "It's my Jason!" And even before she could reach the privacy of the other room, she burst into sobs. Nora took her by her shaking shoulders, pushed her through the door and closed it.

Tessa turned back into the kitchen. Dad was already washing up, Ned was peering at the coffee machine and nodding wisely.

"Mrs Skilbeck's here," said Tessa. "Very upset – I think they haven't found Jason!"

"Better make some extra coffee," her dad said to Ned. "I've a feeling we're all going to need it."

"Oh, that's just what we need!" Nora sounded very relieved when they entered the sitting room, loaded with mugs and the coffee tray. "Now, have a cup of coffee, Mrs Skilbeck, and we'll ask the children if they have any ideas." She handed out the mugs as fast as Ned could fill them.

Mrs Skilbeck didn't touch hers. "I allus have his tea on the table prompt at four," she said. "Just a little snack, you understand." Mrs Skilbeck looked at Tessa's dad, then turned away. "No, perhaps you wouldn't," she muttered.

"Oh, yes he would," Tessa said, indignantly. "He always has my tea ready for me when I get home."

"Shhh, Tess," said Dad, laying his broad hand on top of her head. "We know he didn't come in for his tea," he said to Mrs Skilbeck. "Your husband came round to Delves Cottage earlier."

Mrs Skilbeck's hand jerked up to her face, as if she'd been stung . . . or slapped, thought Tessa.

"Gary's out looking for him now. I wanted to get the police but he wouldn't have that. Says we had enough of the police over that injured dog our Jason found. Well, if they can waste their time asking daft questions about a dog fight, why shouldn't they get out there and look for our Jason?" She looked across at Ned now, as if he could give her an answer. Ned nodded vaguely into space. There was a silence; Mrs Skilbeck seemed to have run down for a moment.

"Now look, what would you like us to do?" asked Nora in her cool, professional manner.

Mrs Skilbeck shook her head without so much as disturbing a single blonde hair. "I don't know. He went off and it's getting dark and I don't know where he can be and I just thought that your lad might know and . . ." She sniffed and dabbed at her blue-lidded eyes with a very white handkerchief. Tessa was reminded of the other one, still in her jeans pocket at home.

"When did you last see Jason?" Nora asked Ned.

He shrugged. "In school." He frowned, and Tessa wondered whether he was remembering the way he'd looked for Jason when he and Dad were answering the last question of the afternoon: Tracey Jones's question about building houses.

"He didn't seem to be around when school ended," said Tessa's dad. "I'd have given him a lift if he had been."

"No!" said Mrs Skilbeck sharply. "Jason's not allowed to accept lifts from . . ."

"From strangers," supplied Nora. "Quite right too, though Mr Gostard is no stranger to Jason and he was bringing Ned and Tess home anyway."

"Not from anybody," Mrs Skilbeck stated flatly.

There was a pause. Tessa was thinking frantically. There was some clue to all this, something Jason had said – to her. But what? She just couldn't put her finger on it.

"You're looking thoughtful, Tess," said Dad. "You know something?"

Tessa hesitated. If she said anything about their lunch-time meeting, she'd land them both in trouble. She shook her head, still thinking furiously.

"Was he all right at school today?" Dad asked her.

"Mmmmm – a bit edgy, you know . . ."

"No, we don't know. Tell us clearly."

"Well . . . he was fussing about all over the place; never came to sit at our table all morning."

Mrs Skilbeck nodded. "He was in a right state last night," she said. "Couldn't get to sleep for a long time, then when he did he had nightmares."

"Why was that?" Nora lifted her glasses and settled them on her nose.

"How should I know? They don't tell me anything, them two. Gary with his plans and Jason with his problems – you'd think they'd got nobody to talk to." Mrs Skilbeck spoke bitterly. "I'm surprised he didn't tell you," she added, glaring at Tessa's dad.

"Me? Why?"

"'Cos he spends as much time as he dare round at your place, goes up the woods with you, always talking about the things you've got . . ."

"Things we've got?" Tessa was amazed. She knew for a fact that the Skilbecks had Sky television, and Jason had his own video and his own computer.

"Books and stuff," Mrs Skilbeck said, vaguely. "Said he was going to help you to clear the garden."

Tessa frowned; Dad hadn't mentioned that to her. It seemed that he and Jason were quite friendly now, walking the woods, doing the garden. Why hadn't Dad told her? Well, she knew the answer to that: she'd made it very clear she didn't want to be friends with Jason. Tessa shook her head rapidly as if to clear the anxious thoughts that were gathering. She heard Dad's calm, deep voice soothing Mrs Skilbeck.

"So you last saw him at lunch-time?"

"Yes, he's always home dead on five-past twelve."

"Was he all right then?"

Mrs Skilbeck shook her head miserably. "Didn't eat hardly anything. Full of hay fever. I wanted him to stay at home but he would go. Said he had to go to listen to your talk." Again she looked at Dad, accusingly.

Dad was silent for a moment. When he spoke he looked straight at Tessa. "I didn't see him at the school this afternoon."

Silence.

Ned said, "I don't think he was at Jim's talk."

"You think he never went back to school after dinner?" Mrs Skilbeck's voice rose. "But where else would he go? I offered to let him have the afternoon off, begged him to stay out of the pollen. He wouldn't, said he'd be all right, said his dad'd make him . . ." Her voice shook.

"Was he there, Tess?" Dad was still looking at her.

Tess shook her head, but before she could say anything – if she was going to say anything – Mrs Skilbeck burst out:

"He *has* run away! I told Gary he'd do something . . . allus down at your place . . . never at home since you arrived . . ." She glared wildly over at Dad.

"So you think Jason is somewhere around Delves Cottage?" he murmured.

Mrs Skilbeck nodded and sniffed and Tessa remembered the last time she'd spoken to Jason, in the bus-shelter, with his hay fever. What was it he'd said that was so important? She tried to recall everything they'd talked about but she felt so guilty about tackling Jason, about being so fierce with him, about breaking her word to Dad . . .

"Right, let's go," Tessa's dad put his coffee mug back on the tray and stood up.

"Where are you going?" Mrs Skilbeck asked.

"To search for Jason – at Delves Cottage."

Her neatly-plucked and pencilled eyebrows

rose almost to her silvery hairline. "No, I can't do that!"

"But I thought that's what you'd come for."

"No . . . yes . . . no, I mean I want you to go and look. But I'll have to get back before Gary. He'll lose his rag if he knows I've been here." She flicked her head round as if indicating a forbidden place.

"Out of bounds, are we?" Nora didn't sound very sympathetic. "Look, you get back home, we'll all go to Delves Cottage and have a good hunt round – outhouses and all. Right? We'll be in touch whether we find him or not."

The blue-lidded eyes opened wide. "But what shall I tell Gary?"

"Mrs Skilbeck, do you want us to help you find Jason or not?" Nora sounded quite fierce and the other woman nodded miserably. "Right. So you go and wait for Gary," Nora emphasized the name, "and we'll go and search for Jason. The sooner we get going the better."

Mrs Skilbeck hesitated, then got up. "And you'll ring if you find him?"

Tessa's dad nodded. "We'll call as soon as we've searched." He moved towards Mrs Skilbeck, towering over her protectively. Mrs Skilbeck threw him a panicky look and fled. They heard her heels clattering down the stairs.

"Sorry about all this, Jim," said Nora. "If you'd rather not get involved . . ."

He shook his head. "I think I am involved, as far as the parents are concerned. I've always felt that Jason hung around our place more than we knew. He's never been with me up in the woods – and as for his gardening plans . . ." He looked hard at Tessa, who made sure she didn't look back. "Right then, come on! Have you got a good torch? And cover yourselves up – our garden's a right jungle!"

Chapter 9

Dad went from room to room putting on all the lights. For the first time, Tessa saw their home as a visitor might see it: the naked light-bulbs, uncarpeted stairs, boxes still unpacked, books lying in heaps. She forgot to worry about Jason and worried only what Nora would think; she might have only a flat above the butcher's, but it was clean and polished and orderly. Like their flat back in town, when Granny Lila looked after it. Tessa sighed and followed Ned, who, she was sure, would notice nothing.

But Nora was opening doors, shining her torch into the empty pantry and the cupboard under the stairs, far too busy to take notice of their mess.

"You and Ned do the upstairs," she suggested. "But do it quietly; we don't want to startle him – if he's here."

She needn't have warned them; Ned never did say much and now he followed her from room to room, silently peering under the beds, quietly opening cupboard doors and nodding his satisfaction when each room was searched. After all, there were very few places Jason could have hidden in a two-up two-down cottage. When Ned returned downstairs, Tessa took the opportunity to get back into her jeans, and tie up her hair, ready to tackle the "jungle" outside.

"So he's not indoors," Dad was saying when she arrived in the kitchen. "If he's hiding anywhere, he'll be in the garden, or the old shed." He led them outside.

Tessa was surprised how light it was still. The house was always dark, surrounded as it was by trees, but once outside they didn't need the torches. What they did need was a scythe; the grass round the old fruit trees was waist high and thick with prickles.

"I'll go through that lot," said Dad. He'd put on his thornproof jacket and big boots. "You and Ned do the sheds – quietly now, and thoroughly."

"I think I'll just check with Mrs Skilbeck," said Nora. "If Jason's turned up we need go no further and if he hasn't . . ." The words hung in the air.

If he hasn't, thought Tessa, they'll *have* to get the police in. She shivered – with excitement first, then panic. When the police started asking questions, she'd have to tell them about her meeting with Jason and then there'd be trouble. She pushed the thought away.

Ned was shining his torch into the old shed but the window was so dirty that he saw only his own reflection. He moved along to the old, cracked door. "Does this open?" he asked, stretching upwards.

Tess shook her head. "Why d'you think he's gone?" she asked, in a small, anxious voice.

Ned shrugged. "*Where's* more important."

But why's more interesting, thought Tessa.

They went round a couple of old hen-houses but there was no sign of Jason in either. After that they were right up against the back fence. Tessa hung over it, gazing up into the woods, thinking of Jason wandering around in the dark, getting lost, falling somewhere, lying hurt. All her fault.

As if he followed her thoughts, Ned spoke.

"That's where he'll be."

"How can you be sure?" asked Tessa.

"It's where I went."

Tess didn't quite understand what he meant. "When?" she asked.

"When I ran away."

Tessa waited, but as usual, Ned did not

elaborate. He leaned on the gate, looking into the woods, head erect, sniffing the air as if to catch the scent of Jason.

"Why did you go?" Tessa whispered.

"Dunno." He shrugged. "Seemed to me we'd spent years being the outcasts of this village, might as well live like one."

Tessa could hear the smile in his voice. "But Jason's not an outcast, is he? I mean, his father's rich and important."

Ned shifted. "Yeah, well, that can be just as bad." He turned to go. "Better report back," he muttered, and rushed off down the path before she could ask awkward questions.

Tessa followed slowly. Who'd have thought that Ned would run away? He always seemed so cool, never bothering about classroom chatter, playground gangs, village friends. Perhaps that's why he kept busy with his work at school, and Nora's Place, she thought. Easier to handle than people.

Well, she was certainly more successful with

animals now than with her so-called friends. Look what she'd done to Jason! Tessa stumped after Ned, depressed, guilty and fearful. She'd have to tell Dad about her meeting with Jason. But how?

When she arrived back at the cottage, Dad was still outside somewhere and Nora was on the phone.

"Yes, well, if you come down to Delves Cottage, we could perhaps coordinate the search a bit more . . ." she nodded. "You're right," she said briskly. "I'll get them to have a serious think and we'll see you in ten minutes."

She put down the phone. "Gary Skilbeck's coming over. And there's some tea in the kitchen."

They didn't want tea, but Nora wanted them; she made them sit down at the table, and think of everything they knew about Jason. She said that when an animal got loose, she always thought about its personality before she went out looking for it. If it was timid, it'd be hiding in the shadows, close to home; nervous, it would skitter about all over the place; and if it had panicked, it might take off across two counties before she caught up with it.

"So, what sort of state was Jason in?" she asked.

They were silent: Ned, possibly because he honestly didn't know, Tess, because she felt she knew too much. They were still pondering the question when Dad came in.

"Nothing." He took the mug from Nora and looked questioningly at the children. "It's getting dark," he said. "They'll just have to tell the police."

"Skilbeck's on his way over," Nora told him. "We were just trying to think of some clue, some favourite place – or even habit – of Jason's that might lead us to him."

Tessa's dad sat down at the table and looked at Tessa seriously. "Come on, Tess, you know something . . . aaatchoo!" And he pulled an almost clean tissue from his top pocket. "It's so wild out there you can almost eat the pollen."

Tessa heard Dad blow his nose vigorously. This was the moment she'd been dreading. But when she spoke she amazed even herself.

"Jason's hay fever is bad," she said. Though she couldn't see why this was important.

Nora nodded, thoughtfully. "So he'd not be hiding in the fields."

"Or our garden," Dad added, grimly. "You could have saved time if you'd said that before. So, now, tell us more."

Tessa looked deep into her mug. "I was talking to him at dinner-time."

"In school?" asked Dad.

"On the common."

"But we're not allowed . . . Ow!" Ned rubbed his leg and looked over at his mother.

"Shhh," said Nora. "Go on, Tessa."

"Well . . . I was trying to get evidence . . ."

"Evidence?" Dad looked stern.

"About Cust . . . my . . . the wounded dog."

Now everybody turned to look at the little

dog, fast asleep in his cardboard box. He still slept most of the time, as if to help his body to mend.

Dad spoke quietly. He always did when he was really angry. "You promised me you'd keep hold of your clacking tongue."

Tessa looked at the table. "I did hold it," she said. "Well, most of the time. You know how he chatters on; I thought he'd be bound to let something out if I listened long enough."

"So you were trying to trap him?" Dad said.

There was a sprinkling of spilt sugar on the table; Tessa traced a complicated pattern in it with her finger. It was so quiet in the little kitchen that they could hear the dog's steady, sleepy breathing.

Suddenly, Tessa burst out, "I'm sure Gary Skilbeck's in on this badger business. And I think Jason knows he is and he's terrified and he says his dad's packing him off to a posh boarding school and . . ." Her voice shook and she put her head down on the table.

"Well done, Tessa; now at least we have a possible motive," said Nora. She moved round the table and gripped Tessa's shoulder. "Don't upset yourself now, love. You've given us the best clue yet." And she stared fiercely across at Tessa's dad as if willing him to agree.

But before anyone could say anything more, Gary Skilbeck walked in.

"I've driven right through the wood and out the other side," he said without greeting them. "I tooted and shouted but if he's up there he's not coming out."

"Well, no, he wouldn't," said Nora, coldly.

He ignored her. "I stood out there, listening. Know those woods, often go up there on my own at night. Know every sound. He didn't answer. Wasn't hurt or anything. Must be all right, wherever he is . . ." He sounded as if he'd said those words before, probably to his wife.

Tessa's dad suddenly stirred. "From what Jason told Tess, we're pretty sure he's up in the woods. Maybe he's fallen asleep or perhaps he's too scared to come back." He carefully avoided looking at Gary Skilbeck.

"Does he take anything for his hay fever?" asked Nora suddenly.

Gary frowned. "I dunno," he said. "He was always taking something or other for his ailments. His mother . . . well . . . she fusses over him too much; you'll have to ask her."

"I'll do that." Nora went out to the hall and got on the phone. Tessa sat and wondered how much Mr Skilbeck had overheard before he came in. Dad made him drink a mug of tea and Ned sat nodding thoughtfully to himself.

"Antihistamines." Nora came in briskly. "His mother gave him one at dinner-time and one to bring to school in case it started again. They're new ones – he hasn't had these before – and it says on the bottle they cause drowsiness."

"So he could have fallen asleep for a while," said Tessa's dad. "And when he woke up he realized he'd been away too long. He was always worrying about getting home on time."

"But why didn't he answer? I shouted and tooted so loud it must have wakened him." Mr Skilbeck glared over the top of his mug.

Nobody spoke.

Then Ned got up. "Come on, Tess, he'll answer you," he said.

"Hang on," said Tessa's dad. "We don't want three of you missing by morning."

Ned grinned. He looked happy, like he did when he was talking to the class about badgers. "I know more about those woods than either you or Mr Skilbeck," he said. "And it's a full moon – good badgerwatching night." He nodded to himself (or was it to Mr Skilbeck? wondered Tessa), picked up his torch, and walked to the door.

"Come on, then," he said. And to Tessa's amazement, he held the door open and waited for her.

She looked questioningly at Dad. "Ned's right," he said. "You just go quietly and when you find him, keep him talking. You're good at that, Tess, aren't you?"

Tessa didn't know whether her father was joking or not, but at least he was letting her go with Ned.

"We'll wait at the edge of the woods," he went on. "Got your whistle, Ned?" Ned nodded. "Right, give us a signal when you're ready for us. Go carefully."

And he gave Tessa a gentle push in the direction of the door.

Chapter 10

If there was a full moon it wasn't up yet. In the woods it was deep dusk and Tessa could only just make out the bridle-way through the dense darkness of the undergrowth. Until she'd come to Delver, Tessa had never seen such darkness; it was never really dark in the city – even in the parks there was always the orange glow of street lights.

For a moment she stood and listened to the swish of the breeze among the leaves, the rustle of Ned's footsteps and that perpetual pattering of invisible things which is always present in the forest.

And she had to fight off an urge to grab Ned's hand. It wasn't that she was frightened – well, not much – it was just that she felt the need to be anchored firmly to the earth, as if she might at any moment float up among the trees and over the valley. Tessa grinned at the thought of her long legs dangling helplessly as she drifted off. She was so taken up with the picture of herself that she lost concentration for a moment and stumbled over a tree-root.

"Shhh!" hissed Ned.

Tessa flushed; as if she'd stumbled on purpose! She was just going to hiss a neat bit of sarcasm back at him when a heavy white shadow passed so close she felt the air current through her hair.

"SCREEECH!" The noise shattered the dusk. Tessa grabbed Ned's sweatshirt and held on.

"Screech owl," he murmured, disentangling himself from her clutches. "Let's go – quietly."

Go where? thought Tessa, feeling rather

embarrassed at having embarrassed Ned. He's no more idea where to find Jason than I have, she thought.

But it seemed he had. Coming to the first fork in the track, Ned turned left, away from the main path, and plunged into deeper, darker woods. Tessa followed close, keeping her eyes on the dirty white bits of Ned's trainers, placing her feet carefully and exactly where his had been, enjoying the dank smell of the leaf-mould he'd disturbed.

But when he suddenly stopped she walked straight into him. She must have hit him with quite a force because she felt him stagger forward and heard his sharp intake of breath as he fell. Ned was too self-disciplined to cry out.

"Sorry," she began.

But, "Shhh – look!" he breathed, lying still on his stomach but lifting his head.

Tessa peered over him and saw that the moon was up. It filtered through the leaves and spread over the clearing immediately in front of them.

Like stage lights, thought Tessa, remembering the school pantomime last Christmas. "Ahhh," she whispered, gazing all round at the unearthly beauty.

"No – LOOK!" Ned pulled at her hand until she knelt beside him, then he turned her head to the right to show her what he had seen.

Badgers.

She saw the blue-white stripe and the gleam of an eye as the biggest badger nodded – just like Ned often did – at nothing in particular. Then she heard a distinct sniff as he lifted up his snout to test the air. Tessa held her breath – what if he caught their scent? She prepared to move off. Badgerwatching was all very well but they were supposed to be looking for Jason.

But Ned grasped her ankle and held her firmly in place. He was nod-nod-nodding furiously and she followed his gaze. Now another, smaller badger had appeared, leading a couple of cubs into the clearing. The two children scarcely breathed as they watched the young badgers romping, chasing, yelping, skittering round on the cropped grass. The older badgers watched too, and after a while, one of them – the mother, perhaps – made a grab for a cub and shoved him in the direction of the sett in the bank. A quick grab, a sharp cuff and the other cub was despatched. Home to bed? Tessa wondered, While Daddy's gone a-hunting? Now the biggest badger – Daddy? – lifted his snout once more, then lumbered off in the undergrowth. The other adult – Mother? – followed, melting into the shadows. Show over. Stage empty. Finis. Only a strange, dank smell remained.

Tessa continued to kneel, oblivious of the damp patches spreading up her jeans, even forgetting the search for Jason. She didn't know much about the countryside and sometimes she wondered whether she even cared. Privately she'd thought Ned and Dad were a bit mad about the badgers; it was the sick and injured animals at Nora's Place she cared about. But she knew that she'd witnessed something special that night, something that had cast a spell. And she wondered whether she could ever settle in a city again. She turned her head and looked at Ned, nodding away and humming contentedly to himself.

As if they were under orders, they stood up at the same time and set off across the clearing to the ruins of the forester's cottage.

You couldn't tell there'd ever been a cottage there. A cowshed, perhaps, or a barn, but not a

place where humans lived. Not fit for human habitation, thought Tessa. But she heard a sort of gurgly breathing, looked upwards and saw there *was* a human inhabiting the place.

He was sitting at the top of a pile of rubble that had once been the cottage wall, silhouetted in the moonlight, his face hidden in shadow. He must have seen them coming across the clearing but he didn't speak. Nobody spoke.

Then Ned nudged Tessa.

"Jason." She said it very quietly, still under

the spell of the moonlight and the badgers. "Jason, it's me – Tess. Come on down."

She sensed, rather than saw, his head shake and Jason gave a loud sniff, reminding her of the biggest badger. Only this time it was followed by a prolonged bout of sneezing. Jason's antihistamines were no match for the succulent scents of the night.

"Come on, Jason," Tessa spoke again. "You need a tablet – and your supper." She was amazed to hear her voice, so gentle, so kind.

All was quiet again; Tessa heard only the sound of Jason's snuffling and the swish of the wind. She tried to think of something else to say. But what was there to say? What if he wouldn't come down? What should they do? She was just going to urge Ned to fetch help when Jason spoke.

"Can't," he said.

"'Course you can; you got up, didn't you?" Tessa sounded more her usual self now. "Just get down the same way."

"Can't. Not now it's dark." The note of desperation in Jason's voice told them that he meant it. He was stuck up there at least until dawn. Unless he fell asleep – and off. Tessa remembered the rubble at the foot of the wall and shuddered. She turned to tell Ned to go for help.

But Ned spoke first. "Keep talking," he said, and, thrusting the torch into her hand, he disappeared.

Tessa was stumped. It was all right for Ned to go off like that, but what was she supposed to say? For once in her chattering life, Tessa could think of nothing. She took a deep breath.

"Hey, Jason," she called.

"What?"

Well, at least he was still awake. "Did you see the badgers?"

"Yeah." Sniff, sniff.

"Did you see the little ones – what are they called?"

"Dunno." Sniff, sniff, aaattchoo!

Tessa saw the silhouette wobble slightly; thought she heard the rasp of Jason's nails as he clung to the old stones, and she felt quite sick for a moment.

"Flopsy, Mopsy and Cottontail!" she shouted, laughing rather hysterically at her own joke.

"Yer what?"

He didn't get it but at least he was interested.

"P'raps that's what they call those little badgers – you know, like the baby rabbits in the story."

"Cubs."

"No – that's baby foxes." Tessa saw the opportunity for a game to keep him occupied.

"And baby badgers," insisted Jason.

"And baby lions," she encouraged him.

"And baby bears."

Goodness, what else? Tessa frantically revised all those boring lists she used to do in English lessons. Not one animal came to mind.

"And . . . baby . . . boy scouts," she brought

out triumphantly. To her relief she heard a giggle.

"Don't make me laugh; I'll fall off," said Jason.

"I'll catch you," she offered.

"You couldn't."

"I could."

"Couldn't."

"Could."

"Couldn't."

"Could – so there!" This was daft but he seemed to be enjoying it.

"Couldn't – so there!"

"'Course I could."

"'Course you couldn't."

"Bet you I could."

"Bet you you couldn't."

O-oh, she was running out of this witty repartee. Tessa peered upwards, searching for inspiration, and saw a movement just below Jason, the dirty trim of a trainer, gleaming Persil white in the moonlight.

Ned spoke very quietly. "Jason, I'm coming up on your left."

A flash of both trainers, then a new silhouette appeared – big, bushy head and thickset shoulders, unmistakable Ned. Tessa saw him shuffle closer to Jason and for a moment the two shadows merged.

"Torch – on the wall, not on us," Ned called, and Tessa heard his voice low and murmuring, giving instructions to Jason.

When she shone the strong beam of Dad's torch on to the cottage wall, she was surprised to see how low it was. The old cottage must have had only a ground floor and Jason was stuck on a crumbling outcrop of wall a mere three metres high. He could have easily got down that, she thought scornfully.

Then she remembered the donkeys she daren't feed, the horses she daren't ride, the screech owl that had terrified her. Yeah, well.

She played the beam on to the wall and watched as Ned set his feet carefully into toe-holds in the flaking mortar between the stones. When he'd gone down a couple of courses he reached up and set Jason's heel in a gap. He said something to Jason, who twisted round so that his toes gripped the place. Then, bit by bit, talking all the time, just like Nora talking to an injured animal, Ned guided Jason down the wall face. A metre away from the bottom, Ned jumped. Jason followed, and they rolled in a heap at Tessa's feet.

"Told you you'd never catch me," Jason giggled nervously.

"Didn't have to, did I?" Tessa heaved him up fiercely, as if she'd have liked to shake him.

They stood for a moment, facing each other in the patchy moonlight. Tessa heard the sighing wind high in the trees and the unasked questions in her head.

"It wasn't our dog," whispered Jason. "Belongs to somebody miles away."

"A friend of your dad's?" Tessa gripped Jason's arm.

"Ow – no – he was just . . . just . . ."

"Just a badger digger?" Tessa asked bitterly, remembering Custard and actually shaking Jason now.

Before Jason could reply, Ned blew three sharp blasts on the whistle and, without waiting for the torch, led the way to the main track. Saved by the whistle, thought Tessa, feeling strangely relieved that the interrogation was over.

As they came out of the trees they saw headlights and heard the noise of an engine.

"It's Dad," whispered Jason. He stood suddenly still and Tessa could feel him trembling all over.

"Jason? Jason? Where are you, love?" Mrs Skilbeck came crashing through the undergrowth towards them, pushing Ned aside. "Oh, Jason, you're safe!"

Tessa watched fascinated as Jason was enclosed in a tight hug. Ned, she knew, would be plodding on ahead, avoiding the embarrassing scene. But she wasn't embarrassed, just envious.

"Come on, my darling, Dad's just up here with the car. We'll soon have you tucked up in bed," Mrs Skilbeck promised.

Jason allowed himself to be led off towards the headlights. Tessa followed, keeping Mrs Skilbeck's white tracksuit close. She'd had quite enough of dark woods.

On the bridle-path, Ned stood with his mother and Tessa's dad. Without a word, Dad handed first Jason, then Mrs Skilbeck, up into the Range Rover, then he turned to the others and scooped them in, too. Finally he guided Mr Skilbeck as he reversed and turned the car round, then he, too, jumped in.

Nobody spoke until they reached Delves Cottage. Dad jumped out and lifted Tessa down. "You take Nora and Ned on," he told Mr Skilbeck. "'Night everybody. Sleep well, now."

Tessa and Dad watched as the car disappeared up the lane. Suddenly it was all too much for

Tessa. She gave a great yawn, followed by a sob. "Daaad," she wailed. "I'm so tired."

"Come on now, little lady," he said, in Granny Lila's tones. "To bed with you or the day will end in tears!"

Tessa smiled weakly. It very nearly had, she thought, as she staggered up the path – home.

Chapter 11

Jason wasn't in school all the following week but Tessa was too busy to worry about Jason or badgers or even Nora's Place. Custard was recovering rapidly and it was obvious that he'd never lived in a house before. Every morning there were messes to be cleared up; every few minutes, it seemed, there were puddles and already he was making signs that he wanted to be off. As soon as the kitchen door opened, he was through it and down the garden path. Dad, Tessa and Ned spent several evenings staking wire mesh all round the garden, though Ned was gloomy about its success.

"He'll dig his way out," he prophesied.

"Not if we give him a good home, surely?" said Tessa.

But Ned shook his head. "Some dogs'll always run."

Like some mothers, thought Tess. But at least, she comforted herself, no one had come forward to claim the dog. Even Dad called him Custard now.

Nora came one evening to check him over. "He's all yours now," she declared. "After my report, the police will be only *too* interested in anyone who dares to claim him." She patted the little dog. "And you're fit and well now, aren't you, Custard?" As if to prove her right, Custard leapt off her lap and ran round and round the kitchen, dragging an old duster after him. Nora laughed. "All he needs now is lots of time and patience."

"Well, we've got all the time in the world, now, haven't we, Tess?" Dad looked straight at her; if Tess took on the responsibility of a dog,

she wouldn't be able to go to Canada, even when Mum got her new job. She couldn't even go back to Granny Lila's every holiday; she'd have to be a full-time country girl.

There was a pause for a moment as if Nora understood the decision Tessa was taking. Ned kept his head down at dog-level, saying nothing. Tessa looked back at her dad, then round the kitchen at Nora, Ned and Custard. She nodded slowly. "Well, I'll have all summer anyway," she said. "But he'll have to be house-trained before I start at the Manor School."

Ned looked up quickly. "I can do that," he said.

Nora nodded. "He can, too. He has much more of a way with dogs than I have. I'm best with the farm animals – and ducks, of course." She gave Tessa a wide grin. "So how's Jason? Got over his adventure, has he?"

Tessa was amazed. "Didn't Ned tell you? The Skilbecks have gone away."

"Gone? You mean they've left the village?"

"Gone on holiday. Jason's not been in school all week."

Nora looked puzzled. "You never told me," she accused Ned.

"Didn't know," he mumbled. And Tessa realized it was true. At school, Ned was always engrossed with his work; he spoke only if he had to, and only about the task in hand. Keeping himself to himself.

"Well," Tessa settled herself more comfortably on her cushion by the side of Custard's box, happy to have someone to gossip to. "Tracey Jones's grandad does the Skilbecks' garden and he said they'd gone away – for three weeks, he said, to Florida."

"Rather sudden, wasn't it?" asked Nora.

"Tracey says Mr Skilbeck's gone to lie low. The police were round there asking questions, and they found some cylinders of stuff in the garden shed. Tracey's grandad said they had nothing to do with gardening and the police took them away. So Mr Skilbeck said Jason needed a change of air for his hay fever and off they all went!" Tessa finished breathlessly.

"Not much hay in Disneyland, anyway," grinned Nora.

"Miss Marsden says Jason's on the list for Manor Comprehensive now." As she spoke, Tessa looked over to Ned with some anxiety and sure enough he groaned, but he grinned as well.

"Is that a reward for him or for us?" he asked.

"Oh, come on, Ned, we've had our reward already," said Nora.

Ned looked up with a slow smile and nodded, up and down, up and down, looking very happy.

"Go on." Nora leaned down and poked him. "You tell them."

So Ned stood up and told them all about the letter from the planning department. The ancient grazing rights on Top Field meant that Gary Skilbeck couldn't build there. Furthermore, Ned went on, relishing the official-sounding language. "Mr Skilbeck has since applied for permission to – quote – 'construct a single-storey building at the bottom of the said field, adjoining the road, for the treatment and housing of sick animals' – unquote." Ned grinned and nodded several times.

"You mean he's going to take Nora's Place over?" Tessa was horrified.

"No." Nora picked up the story. "He's going to build proper stables and a small surgery, and lay on water and electricity."

"And I wonder who's going to run it all?"

asked Tessa's dad, smiling broadly.

Nora smiled back at him. "Well, the practice at Jessup is very interested in developing a small branch out here; they'll be glad to let me take it on."

Tessa suddenly felt less happy. If Nora's Place became a proper vet's there'd be no chance of working there in her spare time.

"But what about the strays?" she asked, feeling a bit like one herself.

"Oh, I'll carry on with the animal sanctuary, but the whole thing will be much better organized – and much tidier!" Nora laughed.

Tessa remembered her own first impression of Nora's Place: a stubbly field, a few tatty sheds and the mud-coated bulbous body of Nora's van nearby. "Oh, Nora, that's marvellous. I'm so glad for you – and for the lambs and the rabbits . . ." Tessa jumped up ready to hug someone with joy.

"Even the donkeys?" Nora asked as Tessa hesitated.

Tessa smiled. "Even the donkeys," she agreed. "I'm getting used to them now." And she went on to tell Nora how Tracey Jones had invited her for tea and a ride on her pony after school the next day. "It's supposed to be a treat," she confided. "But I'm not so sure."

"About Tracey, or about her pony?" Nora asked, and they laughed together.

"Well, I think it's time we all had a treat," said Dad. "How's about a trip out on Saturday? 'Course it won't be Disneyland," he winked at Ned.

"We'll take the van down to Debdale," said Nora. "The mallards had eggs last time I was there – they'll have their chicks by now."

"Oh, yes – my mallard – oh, Dad, please let's do that." Tessa flung herself at her dad and swung on to his knee.

"I'm free all day Saturday. You're on." He squeezed her shoulders and beamed over at Nora.

But on Saturday morning Ned was in a gloomy mood. In silence Tessa helped him clean out bedding, and feed and water animals, and eventually followed him to the donkeys down at the bottom of the field.

"Isn't it great news about Nora's Place?" Tessa could stand the silence no longer.

Ned nodded, up, down, up, down, but only a couple of times.

"So why aren't you pleased?" Tessa asked. She felt rather bold, asking Ned such a personal question.

"I am . . ."

"You're not."

". . . pleased about that."

"But?"

"But there's still the badgers." He paused, then burst out. "We know Custard was sent after badgers; nobody's come to claim him and nobody's been arrested. Whoever they are, they're still around."

Tessa stared at him. "Wow!" she breathed. "I

forgot all about the plans to build up in the woods."

"Exactly!" said Ned. "Maybe that's what Gary Skilbeck wants us – and everybody else – to do."

"Well, we've got Badgerwatch running now," said Tessa.

"We'll never get enough volunteers for a twenty-four-hour guard." Ned muttered. "The badger-diggers could try again, any time."

Tessa, greatly daring, patted Ned's arm. "But Dad promised us the badgers wouldn't be disturbed."

Ned looked doubtful. "Easy to promise," he muttered.

Tessa hesitated. She knew that when her dad promised anything he made it happen but she didn't know whether Ned believed it. She didn't know what Ned felt about anything – except badgers. Tessa sighed: sometimes it seemed it would take years to get to know these country people.

"Jimmy Custard doesn't make promises he can't keep," she said, standing very straight and solemn. Then, seeing that Ned looked puzzled, she translated. "Mr James Gostard – my dad," she grinned. "He'll fix it, you'll see."

Ned looked straight at her. "Mmmm," he said doubtfully. But he very nearly smiled.

They went off to Debdale in the Forestry van; it wasn't as posh as the Skilbecks' Range Rover but it was just as strong and much more fun. Ned and Tessa sat in the back with Custard in his box – and on a lead. They had to get him humanized, according to Ned, which seemed a strange thing to do with a dog, Tessa thought, but Ned spoke with authority.

"He's only lived out in some shed with other dogs until now," he explained. "That's how you rear hunting dogs. But we – er – you want Custard as a pet."

"I don't want him at all," said Dad. But he was smiling. He was smiling a lot today, thought

Tessa. Ever since she'd arrived home from Nora's Place and heard him on the phone. He'd talked and talked all the time she was getting the picnic ready and he'd been grinning away to himself ever since, though he wouldn't tell her why. She looked through the driver's mirror at his shining blue eyes, then turned to Nora, in the passenger seat, looking as small as a girl at his side. Perhaps he was just happy to be going out with Nora, thought Tessa, hopefully.

They parked the van away from the water, so as not to disturb any wildlife. They carried the rug, the cold box, the basket and the bags between them, Ned took Custard's box, and the dog danced along at the end of his lead. Ned planned to spend part of the afternoon training him to answer to his new, now official, name.

They settled all their belongings on the banks of the lake, then sat back in silence for a few minutes. Custard had lifted up his muzzle and was sniffing the air with interest. Nora was busy amongst the picnic boxes and Dad was lying propped up against a tree, smiling out over the water. Tessa looked at each one and felt a warm glow inside. It was quiet, it was utterly peaceful, but it wasn't boring any more. Out there, across the lake, amongst the trees, whole animal lives were going on, and she had lots to learn about them all.

She turned her gaze down to the edge of the water; little ripples spread out from a nearby clump of bushes. Tessa held her breath and watched as a plump little brown bird glided into view, then two, no, three little ducklings followed. Last of all the colourful, elegant male brought up the rear of the little procession.

"Oh, look," breathed Tessa. "Can it be. . . ?"

Nora nodded. "Oh yes, that's where they nested. I've kept watch whenever I've been passing."

Tessa stood and saw the little mallard family bobbing about round the edges of the reeds, dipping and ducking and clucking to each other. All complete. Suddenly Tessa felt her eyes fill with tears.

"Do you think they're happy?" she whispered.

Ned looked surprised. "They don't know," he said. "They're surviving, that's what matters." In his arms, Custard growled softly and his stubby tail stirred.

"They won't survive if he gets at them," warned Nora.

"Oh, he wouldn't, would he?" protested Tessa.

"He would. See those three ducklings? There were seven three weeks ago."

Tessa looked horrified. "You mean they've been killed?" she asked.

"Eaten," corrected Nora. "They've provided food for some hungry creature – a fox, maybe, a water rat, even another bird. That's partly what they're here for."

There was silence. Tessa was thoughtful; the countryside she was beginning to find interesting had suddenly become quite shocking.

"What about badgers?" she asked suddenly.

Nora looked puzzled but Ned knew just what she meant.

"Slugs and snails and puppy dogs' tails," he sang, pulling Custard's tail gently.

"Not ducklings?"

Ned shook his head. "Never likely to meet," he said. "Badgers don't like water."

"So your mallard is safe from Ned's badgers," said Dad.

"If only the badgers were safe from Skilbeck's builders," said Ned, going all gloomy once more.

"Ah, well, I was coming to that . . ." Dad stopped and pulled at his pony-tail.

"Come on, Jim, I knew you were hiding something," said Nora.

Did she? thought Tessa. How? "Come on, Dad, tell us all about it," she called out.

Disturbed by her noise, Custard began to bark and the mallard family scudded off into the reeds.

Ned held Custard's muzzle and whispered

"Shhh" into his ear.

"I had a call from the County Badgerwatch Scheme this morning," Dad began when they were all settled. "They've been interested in our little Badgerwatch from the start but they can only give advice, not financial help."

"What do we need financial help for?" asked Ned in a prickly tone.

"We don't, not as things stand. It doesn't cost money to watch badgers. However, they've had an offer for the Delves Wood badgers."

"You mean somebody wants to buy them?" asked Tessa, her voice rising with indignation. Custard growled.

"Shhh, Tess! We'll have to hold *your* muzzle and tap *your* nose if you disturb the peace like that," said Dad. "Of course nobody can buy the badgers. But somebody wants to set up an observation sett in Delves Wood."

"But there's already a good sett." Ned was looking quite pink now. "So long as nobody builds over it."

"Well, that's just what they want to do, in a way." Tessa's dad explained. "They'll extend it and put in a window so the animals can be studied without being disturbed. Derbyshire Wildlife has been trying to raise funds for an observation sett for years."

"So how have they raised them now?" asked Ned, cooling down a little.

Tessa's dad smiled. "Wouldn't tell me. Only that they've been offered the site and materials."

"Two good clues there, Jim." Nora turned to the children. "Give you three guesses," she challenged.

Ned just sat, wide-eyed and thoughtful. It was Tessa who answered. "It can't be Gary Skilbeck again?"

"Oh yes it can!" Jim smiled, broadly. "Mr Skilbeck is very grateful to the Delver Badger-watchers: we're keeping several of his more doubtful friends, as well as the RSPCA and the police, off his back. We deserve a reward, don't you think?"

Ned looked doubtful. "So long as they keep the location secret," he said grudgingly. "We don't want crowds of townies in the woods."

"Of course we do!" Tessa was indignant once more. "How do you think people in towns are ever going to learn anything about the country-side if you stop them coming? And anyway, what about Dad and me? We're townies."

Ned grinned, "Not now, you're not," he said.

And at that moment the mallard, Tessa's own mallard, took flight low over the water, then skidded into a landing, like a very slow water-skier.

"Quaaack," he called across Debdale Water. "Quack, quack, quack."

"Maybe Ned's right," said Tessa's dad. "Maybe we are country folk now."

"Not yet, I think, Jim," said Nora. "But you're getting there."

Tessa watched her dad's slow smile and Nora's flushed face with satisfaction. Then she stood up in time to see the mallard neatly turn back up the lake. "Look, everybody," she said, remembering to keep her voice soft now. "Look at my mallard. He's coming home!"

THUNDERFOOT by Deborah van der Beek

"Here boy!" she cried, and the horse came at a lumbering canter. The ground shook beneath his gigantic hooves.

Mel Whitby is a milkman's daughter who's *always* had a passion for horses. She can't believe her luck when she finds a mysterious horse in a railway field. This enormous horse is underfed, and in need of attention, and Mel knows she can take care of him. But little does she know that taking care of Thunderfoot is going to change her life forever . . .

**A FOXCUB NAMED FREEDOM
by Brenda Jobling**

She suddenly caught a faint whisper of another scent on the air – the odour of another fox. It was her son, Freedom.

A vixen lies seriously injured in the undergrowth. Another animal approaches. It is her young son, coming to her for warmth and comfort. The cub knows he must help his mother to safety, but it is impossible. The vixen senses danger nearby, and nudges him away. She cares nothing for herself, only for her son's freedom.